To Fight
in Silence

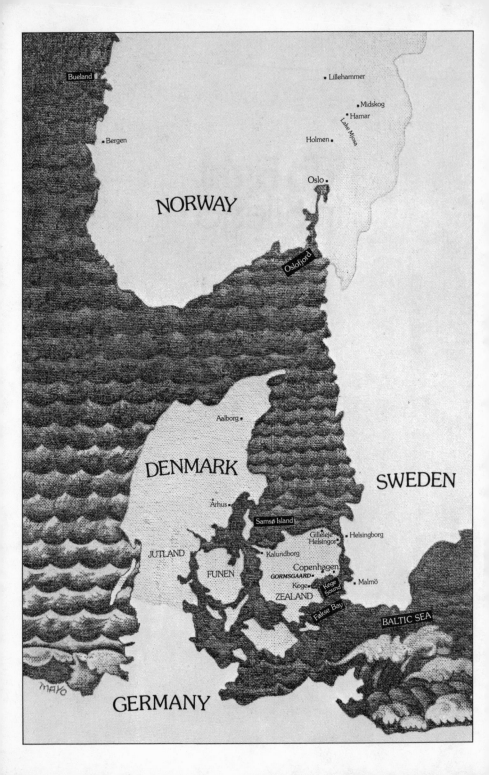

To Fight in Silence

EVA-LIS WUORIO

HOLT, RINEHART AND WINSTON
New York Chicago San Francisco

FOR NICHOLAS,
to help him think of children in other lands,
in other times, with understanding.

Prologue

Gormsgaard, Denmark
MIDSUMMER 1939

When they came to think about it later, the beginning of the strange years was at the Midsummer party when everyone came to Gormsgaard.

It could be so clearly marked, probably because of the twins, Pelle and Lotte, and the unusual sadness that for a time pierced through the happy activities. Pelle and Lotte were small, funny, and you couldn't tell them apart. They got sick from all the crayfish and strawberries Karen and Kristian fed them. Afterward that was remembered as a family joke. Their mother, Aunt Astrid, cried. And the strange thing she said was also remembered. She said she hadn't thought she could have a happy cry ever again.

"Grown-ups!" Kristian said to Karen. "What's happy about crying, after all!"

1

Karen, who was eleven then, had told Kristian, "It's a happy cry because she's here, in her own old home, back from Germany. And because the twins have had too many strawberries."

That was also the first time their cousin Thor and his Norwegian family came to Gormsgaard.

Long ago the lands where Gormsgaard now stood had been owned by a medieval chieftain. Through the centuries the inheritance had been divided and now the manor house was surrounded only by a small park and orchards. The house had white walls and a slate gray roof. At the bottom of the tree-lined drive there was a pond with swans and an orchard of apple and cherry trees in bloom.

Gormsgaard lay in the central part of Zealand, the biggest of Denmark's five hundred islands, in the rich wood and farm lands south of Copenhagen. Not far, for the sea is never far in Denmark, were fishing villages along the Køge Sound and by the Baltic shores. Here in the valleys of cornfields and ridges of beechwoods, with farmhouses and church towers dotting the peaceful horizon, you wouldn't think the sea was so near except when the wind blew from the east and brought a fresher tang with it.

It had been Karen's and Kristian's great-great-great-grandfather who had first built the house here. He had been a big blond man who shouted when he spoke and ordered everyone about, so people began to remark that he was like King Gorm the Old, who ruled Denmark a thousand years ago. His descendants rule her to this day, making Denmark the oldest kingdom in the world. Although the master of Gormsgaard is no relation to the royalty, he is invariably called Grandfather Gorm.

Karen and Kristian lived in Copenhagen but Gormsgaard was second home to them. Their grandfather and his eldest son Axel and his wife Ulrika made them warmly welcome. They had their own rooms and own ponies there. They knew the storks that each spring returned from the south to nest on the old wagon wheel above the gables of the stone stables. There were trips to the sea, and with Uncle Axel to the Jensen Creamery, the family dairy in nearby Køge where milk and cream from the farms all around were processed into butter and cheese to be sent to many distant lands.

But Midsummer festivals were what they liked best. That June 1939 was particularly fine, with hot clear blue and golden days, the orchards and gardens early in bloom and nightingales singing. And of course, this year their cousins from Norway and Germany, would be arriving to celebrate with them. At last they would all meet.

But the first visitor was their favorite Aunt Minna. She lived in Jutland, which is a long narrow peninsula, the westernmost part of Denmark and the most northern of the continent of Europe. Aunt Minna was Grandfather Gorm's sister, a busy happy person who never seemed any older than their other aunts, though actually she was their great-aunt.

Karen and Kristian took her to see all their favorite haunts as soon as she arrived. But she also had immediate plans, as always.

"We *must* get the birch branches cut before the others arrive," she said. "I'll show you the branches we can cut, and perhaps we'll find a small tree or two for the doorway."

In all the northern lands it was an old custom to decorate the house with fresh branches to celebrate the arrival of summer.

Kristian was clever with a knife, and he immediately got busy.

"Not too many from the same tree," Aunt Minna called to him. "We haven't the endless forests of Finland here. I had a fight with your grandfather before he let me cut any at all!"

Karen was more interested in all the new relatives who would be coming. She asked so many questions that finally Aunt Minna said, "I'll draw you a family tree, that's what I'll do."

When she arrived, she had immediately found her old gardening apron which had huge pockets. In

them she carried lots of useful things—scissors and
pocket knife, pad of paper and pencil, string and
nails, and always some sweets.

"Uncle Axel and Aunt Ulrika you know," she
said, "but I'll put them in anyhow. Then there is
your father's elder sister Ingeborg, and his younger
sister Astrid. And their families. Now, look here:

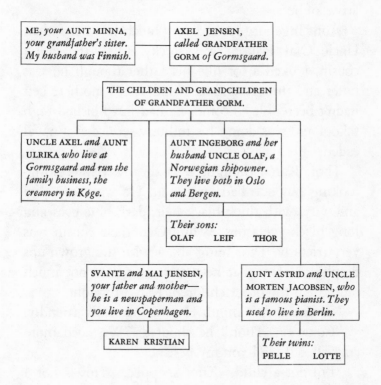

ME, *your* AUNT MINNA,
*your grandfather's sister.
My husband was Finnish.*

AXEL JENSEN,
called GRANDFATHER
GORM *of Gormsgaard.*

THE CHILDREN AND GRANDCHILDREN
OF GRANDFATHER GORM.

UNCLE AXEL *and* AUNT
ULRIKA *who live at
Gormsgaard and run the
family business, the
creamery in Køge.*

AUNT INGEBORG *and her
husband* UNCLE OLAF, *a
Norwegian shipowner.
They live both in Oslo
and Bergen.*

Their sons:
OLAF   LEIF   THOR

SVANTE *and* MAI JENSEN,
*your father and mother—
he is a newspaperman and
you live in Copenhagen.*

AUNT ASTRID *and* UNCLE
MORTEN JACOBSEN, *who
is a famous pianist. They
used to live in Berlin.*

KAREN   KRISTIAN

Their twins:
PELLE   LOTTE

5

"Now, is that clear?" Aunt Minna laughed.

"Yes, yes," Karen said impatiently, "but what are they *like!*"

She found out soon enough, for just before lunch the Eriksen family drove up. There was a lot of kissing and hugging and shaking of hands. Karen had time to stand back and get a good look at these relatives of hers.

Aunt Ingeborg looked very much like her father. Uncle Olaf Eriksen was stocky. Olaf, the eldest cousin, looked a lot like his father though he was taller and thinner and as blond as his mother. Leif hadn't been able to come; he had just finished high school and was doing his military service as a naval cadet.

Thor, Karen thought, was the most interesting-looking boy she had ever seen. He was very slim and wiry, with thick black hair, dark blue eyes and long black eyelashes. While Olaf their cousin was very friendly, Thor hung about with the grown-ups despite the fact that he was just twelve, not much older than the other children, Karen thought.

Kristian didn't mind. He was naturally friendly.

"Come on, Thor," he shouted. "We need more crayfish. I'll lend you my best net!"

"I'm not a child," Thor snapped. "This is not a year for playing about. There is a war coming, don't you know?"

"I don't know what you are talking about," Karen said. "It's Midsummer and there are a lot more strawberries to pick too. There'll be guests for games and dancing and eating. We are allowed to stay up all night!"

"Don't you ever listen to anything?" Thor shouted. "The war is coming! Soon, too!"

"I listen," Karen said quietly. "My father is a newspaperman. Lots of people talk in our house. I've heard them say that we have a pact with Germany. Anyhow, Denmark hasn't had a war for hundreds of years. The war will not come to the north."

"That's not what we think in Norway," Thor said importantly. "But all right, I'll come with you for a minute. Then I have to go back and listen to the talk. I must know things because a clever soldier fights with his brain as well as brawn," he said authoritatively. After that he quickly cheered up and proved to be a very adept fisherman, though he couldn't be bothered picking strawberries. He ate them from Karen's basket.

As they were returning to the house a big touring car drove up the beech-tree-lined avenue. The grown-ups came running from the house.

"It's Astrid! Astrid has come!"

Grandfather Gorm marched to the car and swung open the door for Aunt Astrid. He picked her up.

He was an old man but big and strong, and she

was quite small, the youngest of his children. His hug almost hid her.

"Welcome home, child," he roared.

While the grown-ups crowded about, Karen and Kristian hopped on the running boards and peered into the back of the car, where they had heard a happy chuckling sound. The twins were strapped into baby seats, sun hats tied under their chins, blankets covering them. They looked identical.

When Kristian and Karen had unwrapped them from their cocoons they seemed extremely small. Their white-blond hair was cut in bangs over their foreheads and both wore blue overalls and knitted white sweaters.

"You are sweet." Karen hugged the one she'd lifted out.

"Are you Pelle or Lotte?" Kristian gave a secret hug to his twin.

Both the little ones wrapped their arms around their new-found cousins. They were glad to get into their act; they had heard that question so often.

"*He* is Pelle," one said.

"No, *I* am Lotte," the other said.

"*I* am Pelle," Kristian said. Which made them all laugh so much that Aunt Astrid turned to look at them with tears in her eyes.

"Thank God my babies are safe here," she said.

8

The grown-ups were all talking at the same time so Karen and Kristian took the twins to the kitchen. Thor joined them after a time and buttered himself a piece of bread.

"Aunt Astrid won't stay," he said darkly. "And if she goes back she'll be arrested."

"But why?" Kristian asked, surprised.

"Because she married a Jew!"

"But Uncle Morten's a genius," Karen cried. "He's a world-famous pianist!"

"That doesn't make any difference to the Germans," Thor said. "The only reason Aunt Astrid got across the border to Denmark was because Uncle Axel made her keep her Danish passport when she got married. Did you know that the Nazis came in the middle of the night and took Uncle Morten away from their home? Aunt Astrid is not even allowed to visit him in the concentration camp. That's why she is going back, to try to get him released."

"Father will help," Karen said, feeding the twins strawberries.

"My father says nobody can help just by talking," Thor replied. "That's why there will have to be war —to teach the Germans not to push around other people. They won't be able to get away with it in Norway, you'll see. We'll fight."

But the shadow of Aunt Astrid's tragedy did not touch Karen and Kristian that Midsummer Eve.

The magic long pale night began, the music did not end until the sun was high in the summer sky.

For Karen it was the beginning of growing up too. Olaf danced with her, leading her as easily as he had the older girls. Thor too came to stand by her at the bonfire and, perhaps accidentally, his hand touched hers.

"It will be very dangerous in Norway soon," he whispered. "I'll be doing some of the fighting too, you know."

"You are only twelve," Karen protested. Then the look in his eyes made her thrust a bunch of flowers tied with her best ribbon into his hand. She had picked them at a crossroads at midnight, which was the way to make magic. She hadn't decided whether to keep them herself or give them to her cousin Olaf. Now she handed them to Thor.

"These are for luck," she said.

And when finally her mother sought her out and whispered it was time for bed, Olaf left the group of young people still dancing around the embers. He kissed her cheek lightly.

"I'll be back in a few years when you are a bit older, my pretty little cousin," he whispered. "Just you wait for me."

She would always remember that, for it was the last time she saw Olaf.

Yes, they always thought of that Midsummer as the beginning of everything that followed.

1

Copenhagen, Denmark
APRIL 9, 1940

Karen woke up because someone was crying.

Lights streaked out of the open kitchen door into the long hall. She could see the glow.

Kristian's voice rose in a cry, "What is it? What is it!"

Kristian always slept lightly. He came out of his little room just as Karen came into the kitchen.

Their mother was saying, "Leave it until the morning, Svante. Leave it until the morning."

"Now is as good a time as any." Very seldom did their father contradict their mother. "I may be away most of the day."

"Will there be fighting, Svante?"

"No." Their father's voice was grim. "It's over."

He was standing by the stove, making coffee. Their mother sat by the long gaily covered table where they always had breakfast, her head in her hands. Greta, the girl from a farm near Gormsgaard who came to help around the house, was huddled in a chair, crying.

"Kristian. Karen." Father put down the coffee pot and turned to them. His face looked older and grayer than it had the night before. "Denmark, our own dear land, has been occupied by the Germans."

"We are at war!" Kristian cried. He didn't sound upset, only excited.

"No. We are not at war." Their father's voice was low and weary. "We *were* at war for two hours. Now we are occupied."

"What does that mean, Father?" Karen asked slowly. War was something that happened far away, or in history books.

"It means that there will be German troops in Denmark, until, I expect, the war all over Europe is over. Or longer, depending on who wins."

"Svante, Svante, why didn't we fight!"

"Mai, my love." The tall thin newspaperman put his arm about his wife. "We are a small country with no natural defenses, no border defenses. We have some fourteen thousand men under arms, not all yet mobilized. They have hundreds of thousands. We believed in the nonaggression pact they offered us and we signed. They didn't mean it. They bombed our air force out of existence before we could get one plane off the ground. They occupied all the key points by sea and air. Our navy didn't get around to firing a single shot."

"Copenhagen, they still have to get here! The king will think of something."

"There was that German coal ship moored near the Royal Palace of Amalienborg. Remember? We saw it. Heavily armed troops poured out of it at the same moment Germans crossed the border between Germany and Denmark. Their mission was to capture the king.

"And the king *was* at Amalienborg. How do you defend four separate rococo buildings spaced around a square! The boys did it though. They were issued live ammunition right away, and that handful of youngsters held out against the German soldiers. They held out long enough for the king to confer with the top men in the government, and he was persuaded to capitulate. But the Nazis hadn't been able to capture him, he surrendered as a free man."

"We capitulated! The king *agreed?*" Mai was shocked.

"You know he was thinking of the people. Of us. Denmark was already occupied. There was nothing we could do. One of the ministers told the newspapers, 'We were conquered by telephone.' Talk, talk, Berlin-Copenhagen, Copenhagen-Berlin."

14

"Where is our honor! Where is our honor!" Mai Jensen drummed the kitchen table with her fists. "Think of the Poles! The Germans attacked them too without declaring war. Thousands of them lost their lives in the first few hours, tens of thousands. Yet they fought on, and on. How many did we lose in the defense of Denmark?"

"About a dozen."

"We shall never be able to look the world in the face again. I would rather we were all dead!"

Svante Jensen stared out of his open kitchen window with a grim face. It was a bright, warm, spring morning.

Then he turned around and said, "Get the cups, Karen, child. We will all have some coffee. And would someone make me a sandwich? I don't know when I'll get to eat again. There is much to do. But I suggest all the rest of you go back to bed when I leave."

"Go back to bed! Svante! With the Germans in our land!"

"What else is there to do right now?"

He suddenly hugged his two children warmly, hard and long.

Late that evening Svante Jensen came home, weary and hungry. As he ate his hot soup and a large plateful of eggs, he said:

"You know how King Kristian rides out of the

Castle of Amalienborg each noon at the same time?"

"Yes, of course."

Nearly everyone in Denmark, even people who did not live in Copenhagen, came there to see the immensely tall, bony, dignified old king riding his big horse through the capital city each day, greeting his subjects.

"Well, out he rides right on time this morning! We heard that his staff and members of the government had been trying to stop him, but no one can stop him when he makes up his mind.

"The streets were full of German soldiers, of course. He rode as though he was thinking deeply, not noticing them. Then he saw the swastika flag. It was flying from the flagpole of an official building the Germans had already taken over. There was a group of German soldiers on guard by the gate. The king reined his mount and beckoned to the officer in charge.

"He said it was against the recently signed treaty to fly a German flag in Denmark.

"The officer replied that the flag was flown according to his instructions from Berlin.

"'The flag must be removed before 12 o'clock,' King Kristian said. 'Otherwise I'll send a soldier to do it.'"

"Five minutes to twelve, coming back from his

ride, he passed the building again. The red flag with the black swastika was still flying. The king stopped and quietly said that he was about to send a soldier to take it down.

" 'The soldier will be shot,' the German officer snapped.

" 'I am the soldier,' said the king, starting to dismount.

"There was a crowd of people about, on foot and on bicycles, taking their lunch break. They stopped to watch the Nazi flag flap down the flagpole. The king rode on. The Germans stared after him.

"They were baffled, and one of them said loudly, 'But who *guards* him?'

"Out of the crowd of silent Danes, I heard a man answer:

" 'We all do.' "

2

Oslo, Norway
APRIL 9, 1940

"That is quite enough from you, young man," Olaf Eriksen said shortly. "You will go with your mother and aunts to Lillehammer."

"I will not!" Thor was flushed, tearful. "I am a man. I too will fight."

His father ignored him and spoke to his wife.

"Ingeborg, darling. Do get dressed. Start packing. I think for a time you'll be all right at Lillehammer. My father being a pastor will give you some degree of safety."

He went to the window of the big room and flung it open to the spring morning. Their Oslo flat was their winter home.

The roar of fighting planes filled the room. South, down the fjord, the steady booming of guns made a staccato accompaniment, always louder when another wave of planes had passed.

"Where are *you* going, Olaf?"

"I must go to the office in Bergen. I'll look in at the house, too."

"Why can't we come?"

"Bergen has already been taken," Olaf Eriksen said and regretted it immediately. His wife threw herself into his arms.

"I'm coming too," she said.

Thor shook his father by the shoulder.

"And me. I'm coming home to Bergen."

"You and your mother will do as I say." When Olaf Eriksen spoke in that tone of voice he sounded to them like a Viking chief of old addressing a mutinous crew. His family knew the voice, though he seldom used it.

Ingeborg Eriksen, her usually immaculate hair down to her shoulders, her frilled pink dressing gown awry, resigned herself. She took her husband's hand and pulled him to the old sofa by the window. A sweep of aircraft had passed and there was only the distant boom of guns.

"Will you tell us everything, from the beginning, my dear. I heard you go in the night, but I slept again. Now you return and tell us we are at war. Our ears tell us the same story, but there has been no declaration of war!"

"The Germans have invaded Norway. We should have known they would. Most of us did know, but tell that to the blind and deaf powers that be. We've had warning after warning. Our diplomats in Berlin, our British friends, my own sea captains have warned us. And were we prepared? No. Our army is not mobilized. Our waters not mined. And our great cities are by the sea."

He got hold of his anger, leveled his voice.

"Now we have been bombed, our airports have been seized, they are already occupying most of our cities in the south and southwest. They'd be here now, but Oskarsborg Fort is holding out."

"Young Olaf's there!" They had only heard of their son's appointment to the garrison of the antique toy fort the day before.

"That little old pile of rocks!" Thor cried. "No one can defend it. Not even my brother!"

"The Germans didn't expect they'd fight," said the shipowner grimly. "That is the reason I expect they didn't bomb Oslo. They thought they'd sail in and take over. Don't worry. Oslofjord is so narrow at Oskarsborg Fort that they can hold it, will hold it, at least until the king and the crown prince get away. That's the next move. We don't want any capitulation. You'll see, the king and the government will move north, call the army and the reserves together, and all other able men will join them. We'll fight, never fear, *we'll* fight."

"I'm going with them." Thor jumped up, eyes blazing.

"Shut up," his father said. "No hysterics. You may yet have to, but you have a duty to your mother now. When it becomes necessary to call up boys, you'll get your call."

He took a long, slow breath. He had more bad news to tell his wife.

"Ingeborg. One of my men came for me early this morning. Denmark capitulated. At six a.m."

"Oh, no! All my family, what will happen to them!" Ingeborg Eriksen was suddenly Ingeborg Jensen, a girl at Gormsgaard.

"Don't, don't cry. They'll be all right. There were only a few shots fired. At the border and in Jutland. And the king's guard fought and kept him from being captured until the capitulation was signed. As far as I have heard no civilians were killed."

The doorbell rang. Thor's father nodded to his son to answer. For a moment all three stared at one another. There was a strange new look in their eyes. It would become common in the coming years at the unexpected sound of a knock or a ring. It was not fear, but an instant awareness of danger.

A sturdy man in a blue seaman's jacket and a cap followed Thor into the sitting room. He stopped by the door.

"Come in, Ansgar. What news?" Olaf Eriksen shook hands firmly.

"A bit of good news to start with, Captain Eriksen." A grin spread over his face. "The boys at old Oskarsborg have sunk the *Blucher,* all ten thousand tons of that dirty Nazi cruiser. They are saying at the port that she was loaded to the hilt with all the Gestapo big shots coming to take us over. Instant Nazi government it was going to be, their files on dangerous Norwegians and orders and decrees ready to throw at Norway this morning. Some two thousand Nazis sunk down into the deep just like that, by a handful of Oskarsborg boys with only a couple of rusty cannons to pull the trick with. Young Mr. Olaf's there with them, isn't he?"

"Yes, he is, Ansgar," Olaf Eriksen said quietly. "How long do they think the fortress can hold?"

"She's held longer than anybody thought possible already. They give her a few hours yet. Till the king gets away. The government's already scrambling north, over twenty truckloads of papers and gold going with them. The king's not going to give up."

"No. I understand he's to take the parliament to Elverum. He'll lead. We'll fight."

"Why, Elverum's not all that far from Lillehammer," Thor put in eagerly.

"That's right. Will you go now, get dressed,

packed, help your mother. I'd like you to be out of here within the hour."

"Good luck, Ansgar," Ingeborg Eriksen said and shook hands firmly. "Look after my husband, please."

The seaman stared after her and Thor.

When they were out of the room, Ansgar said, "Captain, if you are thinking of trains to the north they are packed tighter than a can of sardines already. And one's been derailed I hear. Now Old Arvid from Gausa Valley, who supplies some of our ships, is heading north with his two trucks. He could take Mrs. Eriksen and Thor to Lillehammer."

"An excellent idea. Can you find him and ask him? We've only one freighter in the harbor, isn't that right?"

"And stuck there. *Blucher*'s made a mess in the narrows. But the Nazis below her can't get there either. The fjord's black with their ships."

"We'll make plans when my family's off. I'd like you to come to Bergen with me, Ansgar. I must tell you the Germans hold it already."

"I'll be coming with you, Captain."

"Fine. Could you round up Arvid now? Also get the word about that every man on our ships who wants to follow the king to the north will be released from his contract. I'll help take care of their families. I want to see as many of them as possible. There isn't much time."

"Said and done." Ansgar gave a friendly salute.

Olaf Eriksen smiled briefly. A seaman in a seaport was a news source that couldn't be beaten. And Ansgar was specially able that way. A good man, Ansgar. He'd get a promotion. If they all lived long enough.

Olaf Eriksen was having a hasty breakfast, fussed over by his wife, when Ansgar came back. He wouldn't come in but sent word by Thor from the doorway; would the Captain come down?

"Probably something about Arvid and the truck," shipowner Eriksen said, certain that it would be a very much more serious matter. Why hadn't Ansgar come in?

On the windy street below stood Ansgar, his cap in his hand, and Old Arvid, bareheaded too. They looked at Olaf Eriksen steadily, standing like soldiers on parade.

For a long moment the three of them stood silent.

"My son?" the shipowner said slowly.

"Yes, Captain. The news came to your harbor office. They got the word from the fort. A long list of boys."

"A hero's death," Old Arvid's voice shook. "A Viking death."

His eldest son. Young Olaf, twenty years old. The shipowner lifted his shoulders, held his head proudly. "Thank you," he said.

To give himself time he climbed the four flights of stairs. Olaf, his eldest. He stood for a time by the apartment door. Then he walked in.

His voice was steady when he called his wife and his youngest son.

"Come along. Arvid's here. He is anxious to get on the road."

Ansgar the seaman stood beside him as they watched the truck lumber down the narrow cobbled street. Thor and Mrs. Eriksen would be away to the forests and hills while the storm broke over Oslo. Any moment now.

"My wife has heard enough for today," Olaf Eriksen said. "She has her family in Denmark to worry about, too. And us, all this. She wouldn't have left had I told her about the boy."

"That's what I thought," said Ansgar soberly. "She wouldn't have gone. Nor Thor."

Olaf Eriksen straightened his shoulders. His eyes clouded for a moment but his voice was brisk.

"There's plenty for us to do. Let's get started."

Arvid's truck was nearly at Hamar when the flight of bombers swept low above them. Moments later the earth shook and the air reverberated with the thump of bombs ahead.

It had been a slow trip since they started out in the morning. The valley road north of Oslo was crowded with people leaving the capital by foot, bicycle, and car. However, by the time they reached the shore road near the long narrow Lake Mjosa, the traffic had lessened. The lake was already thawed but ice floes floated in the spring flood, the snow melted on the banks. The wind blew cold from the ice-capped peaks around them, but under the tall pines in the forest green moss came through patches of snow, and early hepatica starred the ground.

The roar of the bombs thundered closer. Old Arvid pulled up under the shelter of spreading pines.

"What does Fru Ingeborg think?" he asked. "Shall we take shelter in the woods until we know what is happening ahead?"

"Go on, go on," Thor shouted.

"Why should they bomb Hamar?" his mother wondered. "It is only a little town. Surely it has no military significance."

Old Arvid hesitated. Then he explained, "The king and the crown prince took this road. The Gestapo have their spies everywhere. Perhaps someone has telephoned Oslo that they are here, at Hamar."

"They would not kill the king!" Mrs. Eriksen cried.

"And why not! He didn't stay in Oslo to shake their hands and welcome them into Norway. After such a lack of hospitality they may prefer him dead."

There was a ripping, roaring, earthquakelike sound ahead. The old truck rocked, the trees around them appeared to dance.

Mrs. Ericksen said, "Drive on, Arvid, please." She had sounded so calm Thor felt proud.

"The king must really be at Hamar," Old Arvid shouted above the creaking and groaning of the truck.

"I wish Father could see us now," Thor said. "Sending us to safety! Here I can fight, if I must, can't I, Mother?"

"Yes, my son," Ingeborg Eriksen said. As the aircraft roared over them again she suddenly thought of the little sea-fortress of Oskarsborg in the narrow straits south of Oslo, and in her heart she feared for her eldest son.

Hamar was on fire when they reached the outskirts. Old Arvid got out and said to Thor:

"Your duty is here. Guard your mother. Stay with the truck."

Ten minutes later he came back.

"The king and the crown prince were bombed but they got away. They are on their way to Lillehammer, and with your permission, Fru Eriksen, we'll go there too."

As long as he could remember, Thor had known Lillehammer. In a country that is often harshly beautiful, it is a pretty town, in the foothills of the high mountains, on a plateau above the head of Lake Mjosa.

On the outskirts of Lillehammer they were stopped. Armed men clustered around them.

"Ah, Arvid," said a farmer with a rifle, "you are in good time for the fight. The king is here, and still safe."

A policeman looked into the cab. "*Ja, Ja,* Fru Eriksen," he said. He had gone to school with her husband. "These are hard times. You and the boy had better go straight on to the pastor's."

"What can we do to help?"

"There may be wounded, Fru Eriksen. They will send for you from the hospital."

"And me? What about me? What can I do?" Thor asked.

The men smiled. The police sergeant said, "Change into rough clothes. It will be cold tonight. Report to the Lillehammer police station."

"Thank you," said Thor's mother. "We will walk from here, Arvid."

"I will drive. The captain would want me to take you to the manse."

Small, white-haired, blue-eyed Pastor Thor-Leif Eriksen welcomed them as calmly and happily as though war hadn't swept Norway, and no bombs rumbled the mountain air. He was firm in his faith that everything was in God's hands, peace or war. One praised Him and lived a day at a time.

Thor went like a cyclone through the room always kept ready for the three boys, but by the time he rushed down in one of Olaf's first uniforms, the police had come and gone. The message was that everybody should stay at home, out of the way of the gathering army.

The fight had moved east, away from Lillehammer. One group of German parachutists had been dispersed. The government was staying in the nearby Sandvig museum village of historic houses. The king had moved on. In Oslo the radio stations had been captured by the Germans, but here in the mountains temporary stations were hurriedly being set up so the king could speak to his people.

The pastor turned on his radio. The house began to fill with people, coming to him as they always did when they were troubled. Ingeborg Eriksen found herself busy helping the old housekeeper serve coffee and sandwiches to the bewildered people. Thor could not sit still, he wanted to be *doing* something. He fiddled with the radio until they couldn't get anything out of it but static.

Finally Old Arvid arrived, his face gray with weariness. He slumped into a chair and accepted a glassful of schnapps. He had news.

"The king," the old man said proudly, "has refused to acknowledge the government of Quisling, the traitor. King Haakon has told the government that if they feel it wise to accept the German demands and capitulate, he would be obliged to abdicate."

"Hurrah for the king!" The small room was full of cheering.

"Who's Quisling?" Thor asked.

"He was a member of the Parliament," Ingeborg Eriksen said. "But he has always been pro-Nazi, a German lover, isn't that so?"

"Yes," Old Arvid agreed. "And now the shameless traitor has had himself proclaimed the new prime minister. Just this afternoon. After we left Oslo. It won't last, you'll see. The Norwegians won't put up with Quisling, nor with the likes of him."

"Where is the king now?"

"He is definitely no longer in Lillehammer. He knew our town would have been bombed had he remained here."

The tall, spare king and his fair-haired son had got close to Elverum. From there the king had sent his royal decree that Norway would fight.

Then the German bombers came again. Airborne fleet on airborne fleet. Bombs burst in the valleys. Avalanches of snow thundered down the mountains.

The king and his son went on farther, into the wilderness of Norway, and there they took shelter.

Near Midskog (which means mid-forest), as they had done in the ancient times, the Norwegians who had come from their farms, villages and fishing ports joined the small guard who had accompanied the king and fought the enemy. In this enlightened era the Germans parachuted from the clouds, but they were defeated, as the troops on skis had been in olden days.

Many died, on both sides. But that night under the pines of Norway, the king and his son and their friends were safe.

3

Copenhagen, Denmark
JUNE 1940

Karen stood by the canal and watched her mother strolling from one fishwife's stall to another, hoping to find *rödspätte* for dinner. The stalls were pushcarts, massed on the quay around a big stone statue of a merry fishwife in long skirts and kerchief. Two gulls were sitting on her head making her look as though she had on a flying bonnet.

The sky was June blue, summer bright. Nothing really seemed to have changed in these past months. The lovely Danish summer was the same, there were no ruins in Copenhagen, no lack of food or flowers. It was only a certain feeling. She could feel it right now.

She turned to talk to Kristian and saw that he was staring sullenly into the canal. Two German soldiers, young, blond, in very neat uniforms, stood behind him.

From their gestures she realized they were very politely asking him for directions. There was suddenly an empty space all around Kristian and the two young soldiers. The children who had been feeding gulls, the fishwives who'd been shouting, bargaining and quarreling, the people shopping at the stalls, had all drifted away. There was only the human wall of their backs.

The morning sun seemed less bright. Everybody in Copenhagen had always been *hygge,* a special Danish quality of gayness which came from a secure feeling about themselves and their country. Now in the streets there was unfriendliness. Nobody was afraid. After all, the Germans had been told to behave, Karen's and Kristian's father had said. However, he had also said, "We have no cause to act friendly. They are like people who walk uninvited into your house, sit down at your table and expect you to prepare them a feast and say thank you for coming. It is more Danish not to be friendly."

That, Karen knew, was the least Danish thing in the world! All the songs, all the stories, all the people from other lands said that the Danes were the friendliest people in the world. Well. This was something that had been changed by the war.

Karen saw that Kristian was near to tears. She ran across, reached for Kristian's hand and said loudly so everyone could hear she wasn't being friendly to the Germans:

"We do not speak German. We must go now."

The wall of people's backs around the stalls opened to let them in. Mother was hurrying toward them. The two young German soldiers stared around with unhappy expressions. What was the matter with these people? *They* hadn't put anyone into a concentration camp, had they? The soldiers were glad to be in Denmark, where the food was so good and everything was so pretty, instead of some rotten place like Poland or Czechoslovakia. But the Danes did act peculiar.

There was school as usual. Karen's father went to work each morning. Lately he had started to go to work at night as well, but he was there as often as before to take them to the Tivoli, or to the sea. They didn't go to the harbor any more because there were only German ships now, and many soldiers and guards with guns. There were no more friendly seamen from lands across the sea in ships that carried flags Karen and Kristian had learned to recognize.

Karen missed the trips to the harbor and the weekend drives down to Gormsgaard. There was a shortage of gas because the Germans had taken over everything they could and sent it to Germany where it was needed for war. However, some Danes got a ration, particularly those who were doing a job which was useful to the Germans.

One day an envelope with a Swedish stamp dropped through the mail slot onto the hall rug. Inside it was a letter from Aunt Ingeborg in Norway. It had taken a long time to come, brought across the border by someone escaping into Sweden.

Karen's mother sat silent over that letter for a long time. Usually she read out bits and pieces of news even before she read the letter to them from end to end. She was as fond of Father's sister as he was himself.

Finally Kristian went to her and put his arms around her. Kristian was eleven now. He seemed to have gotten thinner and taller overnight.

"Don't cry. Father will be home soon. Tell me what it is."

"Poor Aunt Ingeborg, poor Uncle Olaf," Mother said and hugged Kristian. She wanted to say how grateful she was to God that her son was still too small to fight, to go into danger, but she didn't.

"It's young Olaf. Your cousin Olaf. He is dead."

It was after that that Karen began to cry herself to sleep each night. She was never hungry. When she tried to eat to please her mother, she felt sick afterward. For a time she felt unreasonably angry at Thor because she had given him, rather than Olaf, the Midsummer flowers tied in their blue ribbon, for luck.

These nights Karen would get up, light a lamp or a candle, throw open the windows and stand there, half asleep. It wasn't sleep-walking, but it wasn't far from it. She did not remember the next night not to do it again.

There were soldiers now, stamping up and down the streets all through the night. They were warned by a German patrol several times. The last warning had been very unpleasant. Karen's father hadn't been at home, and the soldiers wanted to know where he was.

The following morning Svante Jensen said to his wife, "It's better if the children go to Gormsgaard. Their school is over anyhow. Take them by train. It'll be better for Karen there."

"Why don't you come with us? It's about time you had a vacation, and you know it."

Svante Jensen scratched the back of his head the way he always did when he didn't want to answer a question directly. "There's a lot to do," he said, not looking at his wife.

"Are you doing something that's dangerous?"

"Not yet, I'm not." Then he decided he might as

well tell her. He was used to telling her everything. "But this German honeymoon can't go on, you know. We know how it is in Poland, Czechoslovakia and already in Norway. So we still hear the British radio and get the newspapers from Sweden, but there'll come a time, you watch, when we too are going to be cut off from the real news. Our own papers won't be able to report events as they actually happen here. At that time there will have to be another way of informing the people."

"And you are organizing for the time when that happens."

"I'm helping, but the idea was Borge Outze's, of *Dagens Nyheder.* He's been getting in touch with reporters and editors on all the papers, saying that when it becomes necessary to go underground we must be ready. For instance, I'll take my vacation in Jutland and get in touch with people there."

"It seems to me," said his wife, "that the only people in Denmark who are thinking of fighting and offering resistance are newspapermen, the happy-go-lucky beer-drinking lot!"

She sounded proud and Svante smiled at her.

"This is nothing," he said. His face turned grave. "Not like young Olaf. Did Ingeborg write about the other two boys?"

"The letter's taken a long time to get here. When

she wrote it, she and Thor were still in Lillehammer and Leif was with the king in the North. Olaf is apparently folding up his business in Oslo and Bergen. Most of the men from his ships who were on leave or at sea have already left to join the king. Olaf's trying to figure out how to care for their families. She can't say much, you know."

"They are making us ashamed of ourselves," Svante Jensen said. "They fought from the first moment and they are still fighting."

"They have fjords, forests and mountains," his wife replied. "We have fields, orchards and sandy sounds. Svante, don't blame yourself. We'll do our part too."

That was the first time Mai Svensen had not said angrily that the Danes ought to do more, fight and die, if necessary. Svante, who was a peaceful, easygoing man, had realized all the same that while there wasn't much they could do against the Germans in their defenseless land, they ought to stand more firmly for their beliefs.

At last his wife realized they thought alike, as always. He kissed her and said, "Let's get ready to go to Gormsgaard. Tomorrow is not yet lost."

4

Lillehammer, Norway
JUNE 1940

Leif came home to his grandfather's house one day in June. He had picked a bunch of wild flowers in the mountain meadows for his mother. He had his right arm in a sling and blood soaked the bandages. His face was weary and thin.

For a moment they did not recognize him. It was not only that he looked older—he looked different.

"Hi!" He grinned. "The British are already on the outskirts of Lillehammer. A lot more have landed at Andalnes. They probably hold Trondheim. *And I am hungry!*"

"Leif! You are hurt!" his mother held out her arms. He handed her the flowers.

"Leif!" Thor jumped up from the lunch table. "You're a lieutenant! And I haven't even been fighting yet!"

"Welcome with God," said his grandfather and shook Leif's left hand with both his own. "Food! Bring my grandson some food!"

"You've been shot." Thor's voice was envious.

"Only a little bullet. It's better now."

"And promoted!"

"On the field. After the fight at Midskog, Mother."

Everyone gathered around the long refectory table, watching Leif eat, asking questions. Leif thought how there had been Olaf, the eldest, best looking and loved by all. And Thor, the youngest, quicksilver, getting everyone's attention. Leif himself, blond, stocky, had always been "a good boy," never as spectacular as his brothers. Now, as he spooned his fish soup carefully with his left hand, everyone listened to him. He had a lot to tell. But there wasn't much time.

"I must be getting on the road soon," he told his mother. "I have a message to deliver to Father. It is from the king."

It was then he fainted.

And a moment later a British officer knocked on the door, saluted, and asked the pastor's permission to set up machine guns at the bottom of the apple orchard.

For Thor the next twenty-four hours were a nightmare of fire, fear, ear-blasting noise, confusion and horror. The little garrison at Lillehammer which had held off the Germans in April, when he and his mother first arrived, fought again, this time with desperation. The British company of the Leicester Regiment which had arrived hurriedly and ill-armed proved no match for the Germans with their armored cars, tanks, flame-throwers and massive air cover. The defenders had no antiaircraft weapons, not even a Tommy gun among them. Farmers and their sons from the mountain villages filled the gaps in the lines of soldiers.

Soon the small Lillehammer hospital was filled to overflowing. The wounded were carried to bedrooms, bedded on floors and in gardens, in private houses. The few ambulances available, loaded with the most seriously wounded, had already been sent to other hospitals in small villages hidden in the forest and the foothills.

Leif, who proved to have other wounds besides his shattered arm, was by now in high fever. But having seen him to a bed in the manse, his mother left him in the care of the old housekeeper. She was needed elsewhere. She had trained as a nurse.

Meanwhile Arvid had fetched Thor who had been pestering the British for a gun, and set him to help carry the wounded into trucks, bring blankets from any houses where he could find them and be ready to run errands when necessary.

Pastor Eriksen had organized many of the frightened women of the town. Under his direction they set up a canteen in the orchard, cooked and served soup and coffee, made countless sandwiches and sent Thor off to take them to the soldiers who could not leave their posts.

It seemed to Thor he had been running for days when he finally had a chance to get a mug of soup for himself. He flopped to the ground. Above him the old apple tree spread its gray branches, blossoms drifted down. The soup burned his mouth. His head nodded. He slept.

It did not seem many minutes later that Old Arvid shook him awake.

"Thor! Wake up, boy. Can you drive?"

"Of course," he muttered. He had worried his father and brothers until they had taught him.

"You must take the next load of wounded up the mountain. There is no one else to spare. Go to Holmen. Try to bring the truck back."

Ingeborg Eriksen carried one end of a makeshift stretcher, with an English boy shot in the stomach. The truck was already crowded.

"There *must* be room for him. Think what the

Germans would do to him. Oh, it's you, Thor. Drive
slowly, every bump will hurt the wounded."

She leaned into the truck, adjusted a blanket and
greeted many of the wounded men. Briefly she
touched Thor's cheek, stroked his hair.

"God bless you, Fru Eriksen, and the pastor," one
man said.

"I went to school here with your husband," said
another one. "I heard he'd made a good marriage.
Seeing you here, I'll get married myself if I get
through this nonsense."

There was a spurt of laughter, which helped Thor
a little as Arvid showed him the unfamiliar gears
and rapped out words of advice. For once Thor
listened intently. It seemed such a big truck!

Bombs crashed behind them before they were out
of town but fighting the gears and the heavy truck
Thor had no time to wonder what had been hit.
Fortunately there was no traffic on the mountain
road until they got to Holmen.

There the way was blocked. The village square
was full of British troops. Thor's arm ached. The
groaning at the back of the truck changed into a
half-hearted song.

An officer walked up to them.

"It's only a boy," he shouted over his shoulder.
"Where are you going, son?"

Thor had studied English at school. Now he couldn't remember a word, but he had understood the question.

"There is a cottage hospital here," he said in Norwegian. "I am to leave the wounded there."

A voice from the back of the truck translated.

"Tell him," said the officer, "he'd better get out of here. We'll clear the road for him. A German reconnaissance plane just went over and saw us. There'll be bombs soon."

"Lillehammer is badly hit," said a voice from the back.

"We'll go on there, don't worry. But we'll have to scatter a bit if we want to make it alive. Just up a few miles the bloody Germans strafed an ambulance, red cross painted on it as clear as blood. Your truck doesn't stand a chance on this road. Tell the boy to find a side road and get into the woods."

The British soldiers cleared the road for them. Already the front of the column was moving south. Where were the Allied planes? Where were the rest of the Allies? Where were the Swedes, only a few kilometers away across the mountains, with their fine army? No help was to come this day from anywhere, nor for many years. Perhaps it was better that no one knew that. Thor struggled with the truck, drove on, and on, searching for side roads that were not blocked.

"Boy, *hei* boy!" a voice called from the back of the truck. "Can't you hear the planes? Get into the woods, for God's sake!"

A path led into the pine woods on the right. Thor swerved into it, into the ruts left by a cart, slipping on a carpeting of moldy pine needles, fighting the wheel. Behind them the road they had left was spattered with a ra-ta-ta noise, like giant hail.

"Just made it. Good driving, son."

The plane came back, swooped over, the tree-tops swayed, then it went south.

Thor lifted his head from his hands.

"I think we are stuck," he said slowly. He didn't look at his passengers. "I don't think I can get us out of here."

He was answered by several voices, some weak, some strong.

"No one could have done better."

"But what do we do now? None of us can walk or we would still be fighting."

"The farm," Thor said after a time. "From the road I saw a farm through a clearing. I'll get help from there."

He stumbled through the forest, waded a narrow stream now a torrent with the melting snow from the mountains, staggered up the steep fields. The farmer and his daughters had heard the truck and the aircraft and came out to meet him. They sent for help from neighbors and harnessed their horses to carts. It all seemed to Thor like a hazy, fearful dream. He seemed to have been on the go forever.

In the stalled truck two of his passengers had died. They too, as well as the living, the farmers took away. But before they left they pulled the truck back on the road.

Thor insisted. The truck was needed—Old Arvid had said so.

"He is only a boy," one of the young women said. "He is dropping on his feet."

But the farmers knew Arvid. He bought their produce and took it down to Oslo to sell. If Arvid had ordered the truck back, the boy would have to take it. Let him sleep when there is peace in the land again.

So again Thor drove, his arms aching, his hands cramped on the heavy wheel. He was so weary he might have slept again while driving, but the roar of aircraft, drumming close, alerted his senses.

Instinctively he threw himself through the door into a ditch. A moment later there was no truck, only a blazing mess on the road.

He was bruised and wet. He rubbed his eyes but

the tears kept streaming. His face was smeared from mud and his bloodied knuckles. What was he going to do now? What would Arvid say? The truck was needed.

Well. No truck. He'd have to go and report. Soldiers reported back, whatever.

He climbed back onto the road and forced himself to march. His aching legs would have to obey him. He'd have to keep going.

It was late at night when he heard the sound of a car behind him.

Flames were leaping in front of Thor's eyes when he awakened. The truck! Then he heard the soft singing voice of his mother and remembered he had been picked up by a British staff car. They had given him a lift part way. Not to Lillehammer, they were leaving Lillehammer. Then Arvid had found him.

He forced his eyes wide, turned his head. The light was from a fire set on the ground beneath a dark chimney. There was beams close over his head, the blanket his hand touched was rough. He must be in a *seter,* a hut the shepherds kept in the high valleys when they brought the cattle from the lower villages for summer grazing.

"He's awake, Mother," Leif's voice said.

His mother came to him, held his head, fed him broth. He stretched, felt himself all over. Not a wound. Wouldn't you know, with all he'd gone through. Would anyone believe him!

"You did well, son," Old Arvid's words came from the darkness.

Arvid had found him, that was it. Then they had climbed the hills until dawn. Mother and Leif were already at the *seter,* the Germans were in Lillehammer.

"Grandfather?" Thor asked.

"He wouldn't come," Leif said. Leif was petulant with fever and pain and spoke slowly. "Anyhow, as he says, his duty is with his people. It's different with Mother, they might hold her as a hostage to make Father do what they order. And me, I'm just an old crock."

"Nothing that time won't mend," Old Arvid grunted.

"There isn't time. The message must be delivered."

"What message?" Thor asked. He was feeling much better, with three bowls of hot broth inside him, his mother's arm around his shoulder and Arvid's words of praise.

"To Father. The minister sent me to tell Father. It has to do with gold. Norway's gold."

Leif's voice faded. His face was sweaty. He no longer saw Thor bending over him.

"What was the message, Leif? What did you have to say to Father?"

The sick boy tried to focus his eyes. "Find him. Tell he must go north. He'll know. He is needed. Urgently..."

The fire roared in the primitive hearth. Mountain wind whined and groaned outside. To Ingeborg Eriksen the old hut felt like a dark cave, keeping out the hail, the night wind, the enemy.

"Thor." She sighed but spoke firmly. "You'll have to go. Lief can't be moved for days. Arvid Hammer, please help us. Again."

The old man wiped the bottom of his stew bowl with a chunk of bread and sucked it. Thor was prickly with impatience.

"The roads south are held by Germans now," he said finally. "There will be danger."

"That doesn't matter," Thor cried.

"Be quiet and listen." His mother's voice was cold. Would this quicksilver, harum-scarum son of hers get through safely? He was so young.

"Camouflage is what we need," Arvid Hammer said calmly. "Now I've been taking produce from the farms to Oslo for years. I've provisioned the Eriksen ships for a long time, even before Captain Olaf took over from his uncle, the pastor's brother.

If we load a truck with foodstuffs the Germans will
be bound to let us through. They need it in Oslo.
That'll get Thor on his way to look for his father."

"Giving food to Germans! Not me! I'll not do it!
I'll blow up your truck!"

"Shut up, Thor." His mother sounded like her
husband. "Do you want to be sent to safety in
Sweden?"

He felt pretty small. He hadn't brought the truck
back after all. He had been found and coddled. To
make matters worse, he had shouted again, made a
fool of himself. He could see what his grandfather
meant when he said there is a time to shout and a
time to keep silent. All the same, it was difficult
when anger rose up in his throat like a burning taste.

Arvid said, "We'll find some old clothes for the
boy. You can start dirtying your face and hands,
and don't forget the wrists. You'll be my helper—
a dumb one, I hope."

"When Thor understands an order, he obeys,"
Ingeborg Eriksen said firmly. "Go with God."

It was a long, slow, frightening trip, for the road
was now packed with German troops, refugees from
bombed villages who didn't really know where they

were going, stalled cars, lost dogs. They made many detours, were stopped countless times.

Arvid, however, had a pass he had somehow procured, magnificently stamped and signed. Better still was his load of farm produce. Every German patrol that stopped them knew the ever-larger occupying forces in Oslo would need food.

Thor slept from time to time. Once he awoke to find Arvid on the road talking to a stranger. Before he could stir himself the stranger had disappeared into the dark night woods.

Arvid started the truck and said, "The king is safe. He has refused to negotiate with the Germans. We fight on."

"Who was that?"

"One of us. All for one and one for all, as it said in a book I read as a boy. Norwegians stand more united today than ever before in their history. Think of that proudly, boy."

They took turns driving. Arvid was asleep when they reached the outskirts of Oslo.

Perhaps Father would be at home or at his office, Thor thought. He sent us to *safety*. I can hardly wait to tell him everything.

"Where do you think you're going?" Arvid had nodded himself to instant awareness.

"Home?"

"Certainly not. We had word already in Lille-hammer that your place was being watched for your father. He is on the list of dangerous Norwegians. The Germans want him and his ships."

"Why wasn't I told?"

"It wasn't necessary before. The less anyone knows the less he can say. We go to Ansgar's home. Let me drive."

Two small girls were skipping rope at the entrance of the lane where Ansgar the sailor lived. When Old Arvid and Thor got out of the truck, the girls ran into one of the houses.

A moment later the tall sailor came out smiling.

"Did you see my sparrows?" he called. "They warn me of any stranger approaching. Did you leave the truck unguarded? You can't do that in a city occupied by the Germans. I'll round up a few friends. Go on into the house."

It was a comfort to be in a house again, Thor thought. The warmth and the food Ansgar's mother immediately prepared for them made him drowsy. He gave no argument when Old Arvid suggested he get some sleep while they figured out the next step of his journey.

"You are sure my father isn't in Oslo?" he said.

"Sure," Ansgar said. "He may be in Bergen. We'll try to find out."

In the morning Ansgar had gone, but Old Arvid was drinking coffee in the kitchen.

"You go by train, boy," he said.

A train, like in peacetime! Were they mad? He had thought of making his way on foot to some hideout.

"Where is my father?"

"Believed to be in Bergen. Here are papers of a cabin boy. You are a cabin boy on a Norwegian ship commandeered by the Germans. When you get on the train look stupid, don't sit down. Stay in the corridor. Move about. Don't talk."

"Can I breathe?" Thor said.

Old Arvid slapped him on the back and grinned. "That's my boy. Here is a package of sandwiches. The trains get stopped. It could be a long trip. And in Bergen, *don't* go to your home. You hear me? Do not go to your home."

Thor stood in the corridor of the train until he was tired. Then he sat on some cases he found in a baggage car. Someone shouted at him and he stood up. He was too hot and too cold. He felt there was really nowhere for him to go. Being scared was like being someone else, sort of lost. He leaned against the wall and thought of his mother.

Old Arvid had been right. The train was stopped half a dozen times. Once, being a goods train, it was shunted to a siding for hours while another train, full of soldiers, was let through. The usually short trip to Bergen took all day and all night.

Sometime during the night he found himself half-thinking, half-dreaming about his father being particularly fussy about the fish he bought. Quite often when he had been a little boy Thor had gone with his father in the early mornings, before any-one else in the house was up, to meet his ships, talk to his men, and then stop at the Bryggen Quay which pronged nearly to the center of the city. There, from the stalls and the water tanks, his father would select his choice of fresh fish for dinner. The seven mountains looked down on the nine hundred-year-old city, and they would walk in the early mornings, happy, being fussy about fish.

The dream, or thought, was so vivid that when the train finally arrived in Bergen in the early morning he knew precisely where he would go.

He slipped through the crowds being checked by the German police. It was easy for a boy in the crowd of soldiers, the rush of anxious people. That was why he had been sent with the message, he ad-mitted to himself. Not because they thought he could do the job best, but because Leif was ill and his mother and Arvid too well known in Bergen. He would show them all. He ran through the old streets.

The windows of the medieval Hanseatic houses of the merchants were open. There was the familiar forest of masts by the quays. The stalls with their canvas roofs were almost as crowded as usual. The gulls screamed and swooped, hoping for an accidentally dropped fish. The sea su-surred and smelled cold and salty.

He didn't see anyone he knew. His stomach groaned with hunger. His anxiety mounted. He crisscrossed the market again and again. The ill-fitting old boots hurt, the rough clothes itched. He didn't even know what day it was, what date of the month.

I'm not going to cry, Thor told himself. I'll just go all around once more.

A hand fell on his shoulder. An unfamiliar bearded face looked at him, but a familiar voice said warmly, "Follow me, son. Not too close. It's the fifth fishing shack from the end of the quay."

Thor's eyes were dry by the time he climbed down into the hold of the small boat. His father's arms were around him, close and warm. Then they stood apart and shook hands, like proper Norwegians.

"I have good news for you, Thor," his father said. "The king and the crown prince have escaped the Germans. They sailed for England from Tromso, on the English ship *Devonshire*. They have gone to make sure that the Allies send us arms, to remind the world Norway is still free and to lead our troops gathering in foreign lands."

"They sailed today?" Thor said, not really caring, only happy that he had found his father.

"Today, June 7. How about some food, son?"

"First of all, I have an important message for you, Father," Thor said.

5

Gormsgaard, Denmark
AUTUMN 1940

The summer had gone happily, like all the summers at Gormsgaard. Every day there was something to do —weed the garden or the flower beds for pocket money, go on fishing trips down to the sea, ride down the fields to other farms with Grandfather. Karen and Kristian spent long hours beneath the trees in the park, reading about an Englishman called Robin Hood, or painting water colors they knew weren't good enough but the adults pretended were.

Kristian made a good friend of Lund, the village carpenter who came to repair window shutters and odds and ends. He had wonderful pieces of seasoned wood and Kristian spent a lot of time with him, carving dragons and Viking ships, or even trees that were leafless but still seemed to be alive. Kristian "had the gift," someone had said in Karen's hearing. She decided it probably meant he was a genius and would be a sculptor when he grew up, as their mother always said.

It was because of Lund that they met Nina and Torsten. One morning the old man had an accident. Kristian came running into the garden.

"Karen! Karen! Find Uncle Axel, quick!"

"Why can't you find him?" said Karen, who was in the hammock reading a book about Pollyanna.

"I wasn't supposed to be there! He is bleeding."

"Where were you?"

Kristian stamped his foot.

"I'll tell you later. Just get him, now."

"What do I say?"

"Tell him you were coming from your room and heard shouting for help. That's enough."

"He'll understand?" Karen knew her younger brother well enough to know this was serious. "He's at the stables. I'll go."

She had barely said her message when Uncle Axel began running to the house.

Kristian was coming from the kitchen with a jug of apple juice and a plateful of cookies and met her halfway.

He took over the hammock. Karen sat on the grass.

"Tell me," she said, "why couldn't you fetch Uncle Axel yourself?"

"Because Lund was working on the secret room."

"You are telling stories, Kristian! A *secret* room!"

"It's under the stairs and half into the cupboard, as we come down from your room and mine. Lund wasn't supposed to tell me, but I help him, holding the nails and bringing wood. I wasn't to tell anyone I knew."

"You're telling me."

"You're my sister, and you won't tell."

"What happened to Lund?"

"There's blood on his head. A beam fell. Look, here they come."

Uncle Axel saw them and called, "He isn't badly hurt, but better to see a doctor anyhow. Do you want to come too?"

Much later Karen thought that probably he hadn't wanted them to see the entrance to the secret room. At the time she simply ran into the car.

Doctor Holstein was new in the village. No one at Gormsgaard had needed a doctor since the old one retired. There were two strange children in the garden swing by his house, so Karen and Kristian, who had often swung there while waiting, stayed by the car.

Everyone who passed down the street said good

day, good day, to Karen and Kristian. They were used to it but the dark-haired girl with sparkling black eyes couldn't contain her curiosity.

"Are you royalty or something?" she asked.

"Of course not," Karen said.

"Why does everyone greet you then?"

"Because they are our friends."

"Because," Kristian corrected Karen slowly, "they are friends of our grandfather, and they have known us since we were born."

"Only people who lived next to us, or friends and relatives, spoke to us."

"You must be from Copenhagen," Kristian said. "You wait, after a few weeks when people know who you are, everybody will speak to you just the way they do to us."

By the time Uncle Axel, the doctor and Lund came out, the four children had found out that Nina was just the same age as Karen, and Torsten was only a year older than Kristian. They liked riding, fishing, swimming, picnics and playing Indians, too.

"Ah *ja,* Dr. Holstein—" Uncle Axel smiled at them—"I see my young ones have made friends. Please bring your children to Gormsgaard when you come to see Lund tomorrow."

"Why can't they come today?" Karen asked.

"Why not, if their father says yes. Go and fetch your nightgowns and toothbrushes, children. We must hurry to get Lund to bed."

That's how the summer suddenly got brighter. Nina was full of ideas for new games, she could make up songs, and what pleased Aunt Ulrika, she got Karen away from her books a bit. Torsten was quieter but he liked fishing, he found clay by the stream that was good enough for modeling, and whenever Aunt Ulrika was working in the flower garden he was more help than all the rest.

For the children the war was somewhere else, not in Denmark. Lots of adults felt the same way that first year.

Some even said right out that the occupation was a good thing for Denmark. The Germans bought so much Danish produce both for the troops and to send back to Germany that a lot of people felt extra prosperous. They hadn't realized yet that the German occupation mark they were paid with was worthless. They would never get their money back. And not only were the goods gone but soon there would be a shortage of everything and strict rationing of the few things they could produce. But that first year they were naïvely unconcerned, apathetic, and quite a few were cooperative. After all, the Germans weren't doing any *harm* in Denmark.

At Gormsgaard the sun shone, the birds sang, and all seemed well. But the first shadow fell one day in late September.

Karen, Kristian, Nina and Torsten had been picking the last of the apples and berries in the garden. Later there would be a special cake because their father and mother were coming for the first time in two months. Just to make it like an old-time party they were putting on a play Nina had written, with parts for the twins as well. Pelle and Lotte were to sing a song, which was supposed to have been a secret from the grown-ups, but they sang it all day long.

> *An apple am I!*
> *No, the apple is me!*
>
> *Then you are the pie!*
> *You're the apple, I see!*
>
> *Pelle, Lotte, who is me?*
> *Lotte, Pelle, can't you see!*

Karen said, laughing, "Give us a chance to rehearse too. They'll soon be here."

That was when they heard the sound of a car turning up the long beech-lined drive.

"That's not my father's," Kristian said. "His goes

phut-phoo-uh, phut-pooh-ah, because of the bad gas.
This one's roaring."

The big car swept around the curve of the gravel
drive so fast that had any of the children been there,
they wouldn't have had time to get away.

Aunt Ulrika jumped up from the garden chair
angrily. She would certainly give a piece of her mind
to the driver.

It was a big black car with swastikas painted on
the sides. The men who jumped out wore the black
uniforms and the skull insignia of the Gestapo. The
one officer in the car didn't get out of the back until
the door was held open for him. His Gestapo uniform was so neat it must have been ironed only a
few hours earlier. He took off his cap. His hair was
blond and long.

"Aunt Ulrika!" he called. "There you are under
the trees, as though you hadn't moved. Still keeping
English tea time?"

Aunt Ulrika stood, straight and pale. She put out
her hand, warding off the hug she could see coming,
turning it into a stiff handshake.

"You must be Rudi. So this is the manner of your
return," she said.

In the short hateful silence Karen suddenly remembered.

Rudi was the "Vienna boy," the starveling refugee

who had lived at Gormsgaard after the First World War. All over Denmark families had taken in children from the war-torn lands, fed them and given them a home until their families and countries could support them again. She remembered now the conversation she had heard between her mother and Aunt Ulrika. "Svante says Rudi Dietl is back." "Dear God, *not* with the Germans!" "Worse, in the Gestapo." "Oh dear, oh dear. He was six when he came to us, nearly ten when he went back, twice as tall. We cried when he left." "Svante says there are quite a few of the wartime refugee children with the Germans. They get higher pay and higher rank if they spy on us." "Surely not Rudi, he was such a nice boy."

There had been a lot more talk, and one thing Karen remembered clearly. Aunt Ulrika had said, "If he is with the Germans Grandfather Gorm won't have him in the house." And here was Rudi Dietl in the most hated uniform of all.

"I am a big boy now, Auntie," he was saying. He nodded toward the car: "And not doing badly."

Karen and Kristian had come to stand by Aunt Ulrika. Somehow they felt she needed them. Nina and Torsten had backed farther and farther down the lawn. The twins were chattering with the men by the car. They had reverted to their baby German, Karen realized.

"Shall we sit down, all cozy?" said Rudi Dietl. "I've heard some silly nonsense that the Danes are running out of coffee. I've plenty, so I brought you some."

But Aunt Ulrika's mind was made up. Rudi knew as well as she that the Danes didn't have coffee because the Germans had confiscated it all. Her face was pale and her voice so cold they hardly recognized it.

"We have all we need. We are just going out. Children, run and change, quickly."

The tall Gestapo officer's face turned ugly. He looked around.

"Who is that dark girl in the bushes? Not yours, Aunt Ulrika, we know you haven't managed to have any children. With those black eyes she has, I can make a good guess. Not very wise of you, is it, Aunt Ulrika? And these small ones speaking German, the Reich may have a right to them, isn't that so?"

He started toward the twins. Aunt Ulrika swept past him, seized the twins by their hands and hauled them to her.

They burst into loud screams. The sweets they had been given fell from their hands. An orange rolled under the car.

"Please go, Rudi." Her voice was shaking. "If you must come back, come when there are men at home."

She marched into the house, hauling the screaming twins. Karen and Kristian followed her. Karen glanced around but she couldn't see Nina or Torsten.

Aunt Ulrika slammed the door which stood open all summer long. Behind it they could hear the big car roaring, crashing against a bush, crunching into a flower bed, thundering down the drive.

Aunt Ulrika burst into tears.

Karen wasn't trying to listen but her window opened to the garden.

It was an unusually warm evening and as all the shutters and curtains had to be drawn the moment the lights were lit, the grown-ups were sitting by the round table under the trees.

"It just wasn't the smartest way of dealing with it," Uncle Axel repeated again.

"What *should* I have done!" Aunt Ulrika cried.

"What else could she have done?" It was the voice of Karen's father. "None of us have decided how to deal with them."

"Svante!" Grandfather Gorm roared. "I've told you how. We shoot them. That's what we do. I will not have Gestapo scum in my house."

"Father, listen to me. Do you want all of us imprisoned, perhaps shot?"

"Surely! Rather than dishonored."

"Does it occur to you, Father, that we can do a better job if we stay alive? For Denmark and for the people who think like us and who will be our Allies if we show good will. We should fight in our own way."

"There's only one way to fight Hitler's hordes. Die if we must."

"We can also fight with a word. The truth. Resistance in Denmark must be given time to grow."

"Subterfuge," said Uncle Axel. "Go along with them."

"You are my eldest son," shouted Grandfather Gorm, "but I'll put you out of this house if I hear you talk like that again."

"There is a way." Karen heard her father begin again when there was a knock on her door.

"Come in," she called softly. No one answered. She opened it.

Nina and Torsten, glooming like ghosts in the dim hall, stood there. They were dressed and carrying their cases.

"We are going to our home," Nina's voice held a sob.

"What is it?" Karen asked, alarmed.

"We don't want to bring trouble. You saw how the evening was spoiled."

"Because of us," Torsten added.

"But it had nothing to do with you! We didn't have our play because the grown-ups were upset about that Rudi."

"It's because we are Jewish. We'll bring trouble to Gormsgaard."

"We'd better go and see Father," Kristian said, and led the way down the staircase, through the dark living room and the flight of wide steps into the now moonlit garden.

The grown-ups looked up and watched them cross th___ ___n. A half sentence hung in the air.

"Karen and Kristian, why aren't you in bed?" Mai Jensen said. "Torsten and Nina, why are you all dressed?"

"They are going away." Karen hurled herself into her father's lap.

"I don't understand."

"Because we are Jewish." Nina tried to keep her voice steady. "We bring trouble. My father warned us this would happen even here. Torsten and I love you, we don't want anything to happen to you."

"So we are going away," Torsten said, sobbing. "We heard the Gestapo man."

Aunt Ulrika got up. She held Torsten close to her.

Grandfather Gorm began to bellow. He was so angry they only could hear bits, ". . . my house . . . these children . . ."

"Please, Father," Svante Jensen said. "Nina and Karen, Torsten, Kristian, come here and listen to me.

"The reason you, Karen and Kristian, don't understand why Nina and Torsten should be afraid is because you are Danes of Lutheran religion and they are Danes of Jewish faith. That is, we pray to the same God but in a different way. In Denmark this difference doesn't matter so no one thinks about it. You two haven't even realized any difference exists.

"The Germans, on the other hand, have a block on their minds. It is like being half an idiot, however clever the other half of your brain is. They say Jews are no good simply because they are Jews. Pelle's and Lotte's father is in a concentration camp just because of that, despite the fact that he is one of the foremost pianists of our time and a good man. Tens of thousands of Jews are in concentration camps. This persecution is insane, evil.

"Nina's and Torsten's great-grandfather was one of Denmark's most famous physicians. All of Denmark was proud of him, but had he lived in Germany today he'd be in a concentration camp. Nina and Torsten know this, because the Jews have been persecuted in many lands over many centuries for practicing their own religion. That is why they are afraid.

"But while it is very thoughtful, very brave of you, Nina and Torsten, to try to protect us by going away, you forget something. You are Danes. Your family has been Danish for some three or four hundred years I believe. You are not behaving like Danes tonight. You are doubting us, who are your fellow countrymen. Frightening, unforgivable acts are taking place in countries conquered by Germany today, but not in Denmark. We won't let such things happen in Denmark, you must keep that in mind."

"Not everyone thinks like you," Nina shouted out of her fear. She felt a stranger in her beloved Denmark.

"Nina," Svante Jensen walked over to the girl, dark and slender, just a little taller than his own beloved daughter. "Not long ago our king, yours and mine, went into your synagogue in Copenhagen. This is perhaps the only time in history when a king not of your faith has walked into a synagogue. He went there, the old king, and do you know what he said? He said, 'I wanted to come to tell you that you are not to be afraid, because you are all my subjects, as all Danes are my subjects. Nothing will happen to you that will not happen to all of us. I give you my word.' "

Mai Jensen put her arms about the shoulders of Nina and Torsten. "Now, go to bed. The lot of you."

"And I'll bring up some warm milk," said Aunt Ulrika.

6

Island of Bueland, Norway
OCTOBER 1940

"Boiled cod again," said Thor.

"Eat and thank God," said his father. "For nine hundred recorded years and goodness knows how long before that Norwegians have grown strong on boiled cod and been grateful for it. It is our rich harvest from the sea. We sell it as far and wide as the Danes sell their butter. There isn't a better dish in the world to my mind."

The little kitchen was spotless. There was a low fire flickering behind the grate, an oil lamp threw smoky light about them. The windows were shuttered outside, curtained inside. For this moment there was a sense of home and security. During the day when Thor walked on the quays and marketplaces of the little town full of strutting Germans he felt he stuck out like a red flag on a heap of snow. A dozen

71

times a day he expected to be stopped, shouted at, arrested, shot. He had seen it happen several times with his own eyes, once to a man he knew, a friend of his father's.

"How did it go?" he asked, trying to sound adult, smacking his lips as he smashed another potato in the fish sauce, forgetting his complaint because actually he was very fond of boiled cod.

"Everything is as ready as we can make it." His father pushed a weary hand through his hair, rubbed the back of his neck. He had been away for three days. "And you have been doing a good job, I hear."

Thor grinned. He had never been busier. He had gone from ship's chandlers to ship's chandlers, from one shipyard to another, one shop to the next, all over Bueland, other islands and along the fjords. It would be suspicious, his father had told him, to buy too much of anything in one place. The Germans tried to keep records of stock and an eye on any untoward purchases. Even though loyal shopkeepers had quickly hidden as much as they safely could of everything they had, one wasn't quite sure who was a true Norwegian, who a quisling, who a weakling that could be turned by money or threats.

The Germans had been in Norway some six months and in that time the majority of Norwegians had found to their shocked surprise that among them there were traitors. In all countries there are men who put the safety of their own skins and possessions above honor, but most Norwegians could not believe anyone of their independent Viking blood would be so without shame.

"You did seem to need an awful lot of things." Thor was proud his father had trusted him with the job. He didn't realize then that a boy his age, dressed in old clothes, thick sweaters and worn boots like any fisherman's son, had much more chance of passing unnoticed than an adult. This was also the reason they had come to the islands north of Bergen, away from the city where Captain Eriksen was well known and Thor had gone to school. Most unknown boys look like other unknown boys when they are wearing the same sort of things. Even the mistakes he made added to his cover.

"Yes, two sea-going yachts, fully equipped now," his father said absently. An angry look crossed his face. He ought not to have said that, not even to Thor. He must be very tired indeed.

"Are we going away, to join the king in England?" Thor was all eagerness.

"No, son," Captain Eriksen said. "We are needed here."

'Then this is that government business I brought you the message about?"

"Thor, my son, in these times it is unwise, even stupid, to ask questions, to try to know something you don't need to know. It could be dangerous to all concerned."

"I wouldn't ever tell!" Thor shouted indignantly. "The Germans couldn't get a peep out of me! I'm not a quisling!"

His father's face was lined and didn't seem to be as brown as it had been only a few days ago. He sighed. "Men three times as old as you, braver and stronger than either you or I will ever be, have broken down, have talked under torture. Each of us has a breaking point. Sometimes it is lucky to die, but they won't let you die in this new Germanic age of terror. Not until they have broken you.

"You and your brothers used to play sea pirates, Vikings, around the islands of our summer home. But when a storm came up you took shelter because you knew your craft was too small. These days we *must* take risks and our only shelter is extreme care for every detail, wise silence, protective secrecy. It is stupid, Thor, to shout you are strong. Not one of us knows how strong we are when it comes to the moment of truth. Can you try to understand?"

Thor pushed his hands into his pockets. He kept back unexplainable tears. He said surlily, "Yes . . . but."

"I see you don't understand yet," his father said

with a sigh, "but try to remember what I've said."

That sort of thing, Thor thought, was for old people. *He* was young and strong and of Viking blood.

A slight knock saved them from further misunderstanding. A knock could be frightening these days, but this one was reassuring.

Ansgar came in. He removed his cap and stood staring at his employer with affectionate respect.

"Sit down, Ansgar. Thor, will you get him a plateful of fish from the pot. It's not the way your mother makes it but I claim I have a fair hand at cooking cod."

"I've had word. The lieutenant's on his way, should arrive anytime. And XO1 is ready to sail."

"XO2 also, thank goodness. Any other news?"

"Hitler has given an accolade to our neighbor. He calls Denmark *Musterprotektorat,* model protectorate. I just don't get those Danes, you'd think they'd suffocate on their own breath, taking in that polluted air. And don't they say their King Kristian is our King Haakon's brother?"

"He is that, and in his palace he must have envied his brother in Norway, chased and hunted like a criminal but still free and proud in our pine-forest wilderness. The poor Danes had little choice."

"Where there's will there's choice," said Ansgar, before Thor could put in his opinions. "They've always been a bit soft, the ice-cream eaters, begging your pardon, Captain, for that doesn't go for Fru Eriksen."

"What's happening in Bergen?" Captain Eriksen changed the subject.

"Iversen heard on his radio there's some eight tons of stuff we need coming when we set the date. There's a man from those waters I know, Mindur Berge, a giant of a boy. He's been back and forth to the Shetlands already when some people here have had to leave suddenly. Couple of other fishing cutters are doing the same job. They are beginning to call it 'the Shetland Bus.' "

"Tell Iversen we must clear the coast for the current operation."

They kept on talking in puzzles and half sentences of their secret plans while Thor reluctantly washed the dishes at a nod from his father. He wanted to listen but it had been a long day in the crispy cold weather. His face burned. Was it with the wind, the fire? He sat down for a bit.

He awakened to Leif saying, "The Germans are there. Mother needs Thor. Grandfather isn't too well. The Gestapo questioned him."

"But he's an old old man!" Thor was wide awake now. "How dare they!"

"The day after I'd been there. About me. Where I'd come from, where I'd gone. Old Arvid got the word to me."

"Is he . . ."

"All right? Yes. It wouldn't have done any good to go back so don't look at me like that, young Thor. It would have meant more trouble."

"When he was at the Gestapo headquarters," Captain Eriksen said, "all his congregation, and many other people, came and surrounded it. There were more of them than there were Germans, and though they weren't armed the Nazis realized they'd have to release your grandfather or the whole town would rise. It is too early for them to antagonize everyone. Leif, you'll have to be off right away. How and when, Ansgar?"

"South of Alesund," the seaman said and left.

"He's gone to find transportation for you. There are a lot of our boys on the Shetland Islands. From there you'll go where you are sent."

Shipowner Eriksen began to write, checking in his small pocket diary that had nothing but figures scribbled in it, checking the map, the tide charts, the weather forecasts.

As he finished a knock came at the door. Thor had always thought of Ansgar as the biggest man he knew, but the one who followed him was a giant.

"This is Mindur Berge, then, Captain Eriksen." Ansgar wore a wide grin. "The Shetland Bus is leaving now, Mr. Leif."

Another young man stepped into the light. He

spoke softly, in the dialect of the fishermen of the district.

"August Naeroy," he bowed. "I am the captain of the *Aksel,* cutter, sixty-five feet, one hundred horsepower. We make the trip to Shetland in twenty-four hours. I beg to take part in your sorrow, Captain Eriksen. We, up there in the islands north of England, hear the BBC Norwegian-language broadcasts and we know that Lieutenant Olaf Eriksen has been posthumously awarded a very grand medal. We'll be proud to give a lift to any son of yours."

That was the longest speech he'd made in his life. He had used up his words, for after that he just said *ja, ja.*

"Ready, Leif?" His father pulled back his shoulders, his voice was steady. No one could have guessed he was thinking, another son, farewell, Godspeed, shall we ever meet again. "Can we give you any provisions, Captain Naeroy?"

"Thanks Captain Eriksen." Mindur Berge answered for his skipper. "We've lots. Also coffee left on board the *Aksel.* We'd like to send it to Fru Eriksen, as all the coffee in Norway seems to have vanished down the German throats."

"Thank you, Berge."

The wind had started up. From the mountains snow flurries whirled faster and faster. The little fishing boat faced a voyage as hard as those taken by the

Viking ancestors of the boys who steered her now. This was a saga of another age, but no less brave.

"Farewell, Leif."

"Thank you for everything in my life, Father."

Thor shivered in his thick sweater and oilskins. Beyond the skerries the sea was black, huge. He'd had two brothers. Now he wasn't going to have even one at home.

His brother hugged him, quite unlike a Norwegian. Then they shook hands.

"Look after our mother and father," Leif said.

The little boat went tonk-tonk tonk-tonk tonk-tonk westward into the darkness.

The morning after Leif sailed away Captain Eriksen said, over breakfast:

"I was wondering if it would be best to sail you to Floro. You could make your way by bus and ferry to Laerdal yourself. There I know a man who has official permission to drive his truck to Hamar and Lillehammer. I'm sure he will give you a lift home."

Thor stuttered, his mouth too full to speak.

"But, but Father!" He managed to swallow his mouthful. His voice rose in a wail. "The yachts we outfitted! What about them!"

His father stared at him uncomprehendingly for a

moment. Then a warm smile quirked the corners of his mouth. The boy *had* been in the middle of the job and hadn't done badly. He had brought the message safely, he hadn't been much trouble. It really would be too bad to send him off now, before the dramatic payoff, though much wiser of course. There was the danger they might be betrayed and captured. There was the later risk of Thor's knowing too much, though he knew plenty already. He wouldn't stand a chance, having taken part in a near-military activity against the Germans. But he was a Norwegian boy. His brothers had taken their chances.

Captain Eriksen said somberly, "I'll tell you exactly what it involves."

He listed the dangers.

"Good, then I can come," Thor said. "I'll get dressed right away. Then you can tell me what you want me to do today."

"I do wish you'd get dressed before breakfast, like a proper Norwegian boy," his father said.

They grinned at one another.

"I'll even wash behind my ears," Thor said.

Four days later the weather had turned bitter cold. There had been snow from the mountains all day and at night the sky hung heavy. Gulls screamed like lost souls. Captain Eriksen kept saying it was all to the good, no German planes could fly, nor would their patrol boats venture out into strange unfriendly waters where no one would aid them.

They were first at the rendezvous. Then the two big yachts Captain Eriksen had outfitted steamed up. They had been hiding in the islands.

Their crews were large, out of all proportion to the size of the yachts, Thor thought. Then he realized from the talk that the men were army, navy and air force officers who had gotten away with the king, or who had been doing underground work all over the country. What a risky idea to send so many of them on these two yachts!

He overheard the man his father called Colonel say, "I suppose Oskar Torp knows what he's about if he's ordered this picnic. I'd been led to believe the British were picking us up."

"Oh, he wants these craft for a job he has in mind. This is sort of a troika operation. You all, the cargo, the yachts." Gold was on the yachts! Thor thought suddenly.

"Be quiet," an anxious voice spoke from the darkness. "The Germans may be on to us."

They could hear the drum of many powerful engines above the roar of the sea and the wind. Thor couldn't tell whether it was coming from the sea or from the fjord behind them.

"The flashlight, Thor," his father said.

"What are you up to, Captain Eriksen?" Suspicion had become second nature since the occupation. The colonel's voice was sharp.

"Everything's fine. Right on time. Just like London promised." Captain Eriksen flashed the strong beam of his flashlight, timing each flash by his watch. A light answered from the sea.

"There's your escort," Captain Eriksen said to the men who had gathered there. Godspeed. Welcome back."

"Welcome back," Thor said.

They watched the small armada of a battle cruiser, motor torpedo boats and other craft form around the two small yachts. Two lights flashed a V sign. In a moment there was only the roaring sea.

Thor remembered something. "Oskar Torp is the Norwegian minister of finance, isn't he, Father?"

"Yes, Thor."

He wasn't going to ask any more questions. He wondered if he'd ever find out what it was really all about.

But he was pretty sure right now that the Germans had lost their chance of getting the Norwegian nation's gold bullion!

7

Gormsgaard, Denmark
SPRING and SUMMER 1941

Even to the children, back at school in Copenhagen, that first winter of complete blackout had seemed long. The periodic checks of the German patrols had become a regular unpleasantness. The absence of their father, often for days, and their mother's restless worry had affected Karen and Kristian as well.

They were glad to move out to Gormsgaard when school closed at the end of May.

There, immediately, Uncle Axel gave them a job.

"Whether I am at home or not," he told them, "you try to keep Grandfather Gorm occupied while the Nazis are here. He gets furious when he sees them on our land, then his blood pressure rises. It isn't good for him." Nor for anyone else, he could have added.

Aunt Ulrika was worrying about things like tea, coffee, sugar and fresh fruit for the children. The

Germans still claimed there was no rationing. There didn't have to be rationing—they had cleared the stores in the cities and towns so thoroughly there was nothing left to be rationed.

"I couldn't even find thread and needles in Køge today," Aunt Ulrika moaned one day when she came back from a fruitless shopping expedition. Uncle Axel was allowed special gas rations because of the creamery. The Germans wanted him to continue making butter. That was the reason the Jensen family could still use their car.

These days, every time Uncle Axel came back from one of his longer trips, he'd bring with him a couple of men. "Sons of some friends of mine," he'd say. Invariably they were on their way to a "vacation in Sweden."

Sometimes the men were quite old. Karen thought a number of them looked familiar. One day in going through a pile of back numbers of magazines in the attic, she found pictures of half a dozen of them. Several were members of parliament, one was a general, there were a couple of inventors. They too had been on their way to a "vacation in Sweden."

Once when two of them were staying at Gormsgaard the German patrol dropped in unexpectedly, as always. The two guests mysteriously vanished. Karen was just about to ask where they had gone when Kristian hissed at her, "The secret room."

There were several small fishing villages not far from Gormsgaard. Fishermen were still permitted to fish in the sound between Jutland and Sweden; sometimes they even sailed eastward to the wider waters of the Baltic. The "vacationers" would "get a lift" in one of these boats. Sometimes Swedish motor launches came across to fetch them.

"Better make hay while the sun shines, to quote the British," Karen heard one elderly, dignified gentleman say to Uncle Axel as they drove down to the tiny port of Liselund, on the island of Mon, one early summer evening. "This honeymoon is almost over. They already suspect what's happening. Any day the boom will drop and the controls will be so strict the smallest sardine caught in the nets will have to have papers in triplicate." Uncle Axel, looking like a tramp in his fishing clothes, came near to saluting.

"The best of luck, sir." He shook hands. "After the war!"

"May it be soon."

"Welcome back."

Karen and Kristian had learned even in this short time not to ask questions, but they knew. All these people going on "vacation in Sweden" weren't going to come back until after the Germans were defeated. What were they going to do until then in Sweden? Sweden wasn't even in the war, Karen realized. It seemed rather a cowardly thing to leave Denmark when Denmark was occupied by the enemy.

"There must be something more to it than that," Kristian said that night. "I'll find out."

Karen knew he would. He had the oddest friends, not his age at all—the old carpenter, fishermen, delivery boys, the retired pastor, the woman writer who lived in a cottage on the dunes. Everywhere they went Kristian seemed to know someone. No one could figure out where he had met them, or when. He just had.

Next afternoon when he wandered home Torsten was fishing in the pond and Karen and Nina were searching for wild flowers for their collection. He came up to them looking glum.

"About yesterday, and all those 'vacationers' Uncle Axel keeps bringing home and putting on boats," he said. "The younger ones are joining the Free Norwegian Forces in training there, in Sweden. When there are enough of us, I expect there'll be a Free Danish Force too."

"But nobody is fighting in Sweden!" Karen cried.

"When they are trained they go on to England. I wasn't told how, but I expect they must be flown out."

"How about the old men who have sailed away? They can't become sailors or soldiers or airmen."

"Oh, them," Kristian said. "They are important men who go on to England and America to tell the people there that Denmark really isn't pro-German though it might look like that now."

"That's splendid, isn't it?" Karen said.

"Oh, I don't know." Kristian was still frowning. "The king will be left all alone if all the members of government, and everyone else, scuttle off somewhere else. He can't run things by himself. This is a democratic royal country."

"I still don't see why you are being so grumpy," Karen said.

"I also heard that there won't be any bonfires at Midsummer this year," Kristian blurted out.

Even Torsten stopped fishing. He looked astonished and said, "There have been bonfires in Denmark at Midsummer for thousands of years. I've read about it. Way back in the pagan times."

"Let's go and ask Uncle Axel," suggested Karen.

Grandfather Gorm, Uncle Axel and Aunt Ulrika were in the little sitting room having their usual afternoon cup of coffee. "We'll drink it as long as we have it," Grandfather had said. "Then we go without."

"Yes, it is true," Uncle Axel regretfully replied to the children. "The Germans have forbidden bonfires this year." Grandfather Gorm stormed and said he would light them all over the fields and lands and headlands and even on the island he owned on the sound.

"Svante and I have been thinking the children need a summer trip," Uncle Axel said mildly. "We thought a good time to go would be at Midsummer."

Aunt Ulrika saw the glum faces of Nina and Torsten, and glanced at her husband.

"Nina and Torsten are coming too," Uncle Axel said. "Tell your parents it's educational, they'll let you come. We'll go to Helsingor."

"Hamlet's castle," said Torsten eagerly. "Of course it really wasn't, but the English Shakespeare did make it more Hamlet's castle than it would have been if it really was."

"Is it safe for the children?" asked Grandfather Gorm bluntly.

"This year yes. Next year, maybe not."

With everything packed in, and four children and three grown-ups, there was still plenty of room in Uncle Axel's big old touring car.

By noon there was the blue view of water ahead. Then a small cobbled street where they stopped by a red brick house. A surprise! Aunt Minna came out, laughing, hugging everybody.

"Come in, come in," she said. "I've got hot soup ready. Then get out your warm clothes, it'll be cold by the sound."

"Perhaps a ghost will walk tonight," said Torsten, sounding happy, which was unusual for him. "Perhaps even Hamlet will come and shout out the poems the Englishman wrote for him. Or we might hear Holger Danske, the ancient king, singing and fighting with his knights in the deep dungeons."

"Who can tell," said Aunt Minna, "everything is possible."

"What are you doing here, nicest of aunts?" asked Mai Jensen. "I thought you were at home in Jutland!"

"I'm on Svante's business, child," said Aunt Minna. "He is good and brave. I am proud of him, and so should you be too."

It was nearly midnight when they left the little house belonging to an old friend of Aunt Minna's.

They stumbled on the unfamiliar cobblestones in the dark narrow streets. Then there were the ramparts. Above loomed the huge silhouette of a ruined tower, the walls black against the dark blue northern sky. There seemed to be a lot of people going the same way. But no light, torch or candle showed anywhere.

They climbed from the castle yard, up the grassy embankment onto the top of the walls.

"*Oooooh!*" Not even the Germans could have stopped the sound of the children's surprise.

Across the black water up and down the shores of Sweden there were bonfires. Hundreds of them. Some looked like heaps of glowing red coal. Some flamed high like torches dunked in tar. Right across in the neighboring city of Helsingborg, only two and a half miles away, the fires flamed the brightest. But up and down the coast, as far as one could see, there were more..

"What is it? What's happening?" Karen asked, tears unaccountably running down her cheeks.

"Our Swedish friends send us Midsummer's Eve greetings," said her father.

8

Norway
WINTER 1941

Thor couldn't see out of the train windows patterned with frost and swept by snow. The uneven klinkety-klankety of the wheels broke into grumbles and shrieks; frozen rails met the wheels like a sharp file. Thor was uncomfortable in the crowded carriage. He didn't want to see his father.

It hadn't been *his* fault. He had done just what any true Norwegian would do.

He wished himself back to the small fishing village on the fjord where he had spent the summer in hiding. The ragged mountains climbed behind it. The sea and air smelled of salt and fish. Fish on the stakes, on the quays, in baskets. They had had a small white cottage in the upper village, a little garden in front of it catching the sun, geraniums on the windowsill. On the square was a small white wooden church, and below the square, rimming the edge of the fjord, the fishermen's houses with their low hanging eaves, cozy kitchens. After the Germans put a curfew on the fishing boats, his friend Sverre and he had climbed the meadows under the peaks and spent nights at the *seter*. The sunsets to the west were splendid.

It was late summer when his mother came back from one of her trips. She looked tired but happy. Leif was safe.

Father had gotten the news, however news came nowadays. It must have been by secret radio transmitters between Norway and England. It was forbidden to listen to the BBC, even to *have* a radio, but that's how Leif's message must have come.

His mother had come back over the mountains, climbing, walking, by bus, rowboat, fishing boat, back from his father. Thor thought she must be carrying some messages, not making the long trips just to visit him. He had begged to be allowed to help, but he had always been told, not yet, you are behind in your studies.

He was happy of course that Leif was safe, but it made him feel worse about not doing something against the Germans himself. Leif had gotten to Shetland Islands. From there he had flown to London, and the king had remembered him and his father. Then he had been sent to Canada where a lot of Norwegian boys were already training in a place called Lille Norge in Toronto. Leif had sent a special message, "Tell Thor to study. He'll be needed, for the war may last longer than we think. He won't be allowed to train as a pilot without his lyceum certificate."

It sounded like Leif, serious and earnest.

Leif in a plane, doing something, Olaf a dead hero. Thor was restless all that day, and that night he sneaked out and painted a V for Victory sign on the wall of the German police quarters. He had borrowed the paint from a shed, but when he brought it back he had forgotten to clean and dry the brush. The man who owned it had been arrested by the Germans.

He had been released a few days later, but he had been beaten so badly that he had been in bed ever since. Thor had felt badly about it, but he was glad the Germans had seen the V sign and been angry.

The next time, he decided, he wouldn't get anyone else into trouble. So he went out and bought a can of paint for himself, and a brush, and hid them in the woodshed. One night he decided to go and paint a few more signs. His mother caught him. She made him admit that it had been he the first time as well.

She hadn't been proud of him as he half expected. She had marched him to a meeting of the pastor, the schoolmaster, some of the older fishermen and the village elders. They all said that when action was to be taken against the enemy it would be taken by all planning together and agreeing that the results were worth the inevitable reprisals, not by an irresponsible boy who let another man suffer for his foolishness.

"We are sorry, Fru Eriksen," they said, "but your son will have to take his punishment."

It was the man who had been beaten by the Germans who spoke up for Thor. "Let the boy go. He had the right instinct but bad judgment. Let him go this time for the sake of his father, and his brothers. But it will be better for him and his brave mother to leave here. Discipline yourself, Thor Eriksen."

Thor didn't like to remember that meeting.

That was when they returned to Lillehammer.

It had been a long dark autumn, the second autumn of occupation, rushing toward the sunless days of winter. He had worn the green leaf in his button hole to show he served the king. Everyone did of course. His mother had knitted him a woolen cap in red, white and blue, the RAF colors. That was really children's stuff, he thought, but he went along with it. He had been bored with school and not done too well despite the fact that he had put on a spurt of study every now and then because of Leif's message.

It was after Christmas, late one night, that the stranger came to the back door. He wore an assortment of clothing, none of which quite fit him, and his Norwegian had a peculiar accent. Thor's mother and he had a strange exchange of greetings, after which he relaxed.

"Thank God. I was getting scared because I couldn't find anyone."

"We aren't very safe either. I'm sorry. Sit down and have something to eat. I'll go and find you clothes that will fit a little better."

The stranger ate and changed. Then they all sat by the fire in the pastor's study, talking until late. Arvid and one of his sons arrived too. Their visitor explained his accented Norwegian. "I'm Canadian, but my Mum and Dad came from Norway. That's why I got on this job, dropping supplies. The drop went all right, but then I had some engine trouble. I've been coming down the hills ever since. Fine, hospitable people you have here."

Johnny the Canadian told them of Allied defeats and victories. He wasn't like the German radio, recording only German victories. He said, "We've been losing more than winning, but the thing's on the turn. The air force in England is getting bigger every minute, there's a Canadian, a guy called Beaverbrook, in charge of that now. There are underground fighters in the occupied countries, and a lot of people escaping to join us. We'll win in the end. No doubt about that at all."

Then Johnny spoke about a freighter that had come into the harbor of Halifax, on the east coast of Canada.

"It was the strangest thing, there was this old freighter, with two smart, big sea-going yachts on board her. So spic and span you could have sailed them away that minute."

"What did they look like?" Thor asked. He thought he knew. "But why send them on board a freighter?"

Johnny described as best he could. "The story we had in Canada was that that's how the Norwegian gold, the treasure of the government and your king, crossed the Atlantic. That's the money that is paying for the training of your air force now."

"It seems a very odd way to go about it," said the old pastor.

"Don't you see, sir, it was very smart. All the convoys are hunted by German subs. If that freighter had been torpedoed those two little boats would still have swum right on to Canada. Double chance, see?"

"Is it true?" Thor asked, breathless. He had been *part* of it!

"It's true enough!" Then Johnny said, "And now, ma'am, how do I get out? I've still got a job to do."

That was when Thor's mother sent him to bed. Like a child! He stormed into his room, furious. After all, he had been part of it! He had helped then. He could have helped now too! He couldn't contain himself. He got his boots and jacket from the hall behind the kitchen, the things he needed from the storehouse, and hurled himself into the snowstorm outside.

If you listened for the patrols you knew that another one wouldn't be by for another twenty minutes. Not on a night like this. It gave him plenty of time to whitewash a big V for Victory on the door of the Gestapo building, and another one, and another one, wherever he found a door free of snow.

After all, there was something to celebrate. The Germans might not know there had been a victory, even if far away. The Norwegians were awake. And he had been part of it! *He* would celebrate!

That had been last night. At dawn his mother had come into his room. She had found his snow-sodden boots. Arvid's son had seen the signs in town.

"Get up." He had never heard her use that voice. "Pack. You don't deserve to get away with it, but you are leaving immediately."

"What's it all about?" said Thor drowsily, knowing full well.

"You'll get on the Oslo train at the station below Lillehammer. One of Arvid's sons will ski down with you. Go to the great-aunts. Your father will know you are coming."

"But Mother, it was only to let the Germans know we'd won a victory over them."

"You alerted them with your idiot thoughtlessness. I don't know if we can get Johnny the Canadian away now. The Germans will be everywhere."

At the last moment she hugged him. She was crying.

Klikkety-klakkety-schreech went the train. They would be in Oslo soon. There had been no trouble. It had been a freezing night and the Germans hadn't bothered much about the small group of farming people traveling with their goods to sell in Oslo. The other cars were full of German troops going on leave.

Thor had been brooding, so sunk into himself and his fear of what his father was going to say that he had hardly noticed the people in the carriage. Now he heard someone talking.

"I'll tell you a true story." The man glanced over his shoulder, instinctive movement these days. "It's very patriotic to have a cold. Why? You know that we're only shown German propaganda in the movies now, and everything is verboten; sighing, verboten; coughing, verboten; blowing your nose, clearing your throat, spitting. But who can control a cold?"

"Is it verboten to breathe?"

"Of course. I've already painted a sign. Verboten —for Germans and quislings to breathe Norwegian air."

"Do you know why the Germans canceled those stamps with the picture of Vidkun Quisling on them? Because they were afraid all of us would spit on the wrong side."

"Let me tell you another one . . ."

But by then they were pulling into the station and everyone was getting up, caring for their own families, some with fear on their faces, wondering if they could get through the police control.

Fear flooded Thor too. He could hear the high German voices shouting their orders on the platform. He picked up his two suitcases—why had his mother packed so many things for him, just to go to Oslo? As he came down the steps of the carriage, Ansgar appeared, snatched one of his cases and beckoned. There was not the usual mild smile on his face. There was not even a word of welcome.

He led the way across the tracks, along the dark sheds, through a jungle of lanes behind the station. Silent, they walked the unlit streets, taking a long way around to skirt the markets and the squares, to the great-aunts' home.

There, too, Ansgar led him by the back way.

"Your father's waiting for you."

"Aren't you coming too?"

"Go on up. Just for once do what you are told."

Thor carried his suitcases up, resting often; he didn't want to arrive. He stood a long time before he rang the bell.

The aunts came to him in a rush, smelling of musty lavender, twittering, hugging him. Perhaps everything was going to be all right.

The library door opened. His father beckoned him. The aunts left them together.

They were alone and it was just as dreadful as Thor had expected. It seemed a very long time before his father spoke.

"Will you never understand that none of us fight alone? All of us are responsible to every other Norwegian for everything we do. You are going to Sweden tonight. You are dangerous to those of us who fight in Norway. The men who are my comrades have decided to give you this chance because you are your mother's son, perhaps the last one alive."

"Father."

"Yes, my son. I love you. Study hard, work hard, come back when you can control yourself."

"Mother?"

"She knew I would try to send you to Sweden."

"But why, Father?"

"Thor, during the night, while you slept after your painting adventure, the Canadian pilot was moving out, led by Per, one of Arvid's sons. The German patrol saw your handiwork. They alerted the garrison—the paint was still wet, they thought they'd catch the culprit. They caught Johnny and Per instead. The fault is yours. I must try to save them. I do not wish their death on the head of my son."

"*Must* I go? I'll try to do better."

"Farewell, my son. Here is Ansgar. He will show you the way."

Thor ran to his father. For a moment the strong arms were around him.

"Go with God, boy. Come back to defend our land."

Thor stumbled down the long flights of dark stairs.

Finally Ansgar put a hand on his shoulder.

"Stop sniffling, young Eriksen. Remember your brothers. Remember too, everyone makes mistakes but after a time they take care not to make the same mistakes. Now come. You'll be in Sweden in the morning. You'll travel in an oil drum. We've got it fixed."

"I don't want to go."

"You go, so you can come back and fight like a man."

That is how Thor was sent to exile into neutral Sweden.

He felt a stranger in the Swedish home where he lodged, at school he made no friends for he could not resist the temptation to speak loudly of Norway's war and Sweden's peace, and six months later when he was accepted into the school for Norwegian cadets he was no happier. The discipline was strict and the hours of training were long. Many young men left to fight in the Free Norway forces on battlefields, the air and the sea, all over the fighting world, but Thor because of his youth had to stay behind.

He had a lot of time to think, and little by little he began to grow up.

9

Jutland, Denmark
SUMMER 1942

The gate creaked and Aunt Minna told herself that she really ought to oil the hinges. Then she argued aloud that after all, the groan of the hinges was as good as having a dog—she knew someone was coming before they got there. Living alone much of the time she often had conversations with herself.

"I'll have time to pop this into the oven," she said, "before I go to see who's coming and what they want."

"If it's your fish and potato pie, I want it," an almost familiar voice said at the kitchen door.

Aunt Minna nearly dropped the dish. Carefully she set it on the table and said to herself, "It can't be. I just think I'm hearing his voice because he's on my mind so much."

Hands went over her eyes and the voice said, "If it isn't your dear boy, who do you think it is?"

"Thor! It can't be!"

The heavy feeling in his heart and throat lifted for the first time in a year and a half. The fear that had kept step with him on his trip receded. Here at Aunt Minna's in Jutland, he felt at home again at long last.

"How you have grown! How tall you are! Kind God, how *thin* you are." Aunt Minna held him at arms' length, then hugged him again. "And what, may I ask, are you doing here?"

"I escaped." Thor grinned. It wasn't a confident grin.

"You don't escape from a country at peace to a country at war," Aunt Minna said sharply.

"Denmark's not at war," Thor said contemptuously. "Just occupied and lying down under it."

"You are welcome, Thor, and you know it. I love you and you know that too. But don't talk about something you know nothing about or I shall be angry."

"All right." He rested his hands on the kitchen table. All he really wanted was to lie down. How tired he was! Aunt Minna glanced at him sharply.

"Sit down, dear. When did you last eat? It *is* a fish and potato pie; Knut Petersen brought me a fish this morning, bless him. But it won't be ready for an hour, so sandwiches and milk for now. Tell me everything."

She buttered some bread, cut up cheese and tomatoes and got out the pickled herring. Thor watched her, leaning his chin in his hands.

"There hasn't been butter for Norwegians in Norway for ages."

Aunt Minna poured him a second mug of milk.

"The last time I heard from your mother you were in Sweden. You were supposed to be in a training school for Norwegian officers-to-be."

Thor bit into his sandwich, choked, and started again, slower. For two days he had had hardly anything to eat, traveling rough, hiding.

"They said I had to stay until I was eighteen. I'm past fifteen now and there's a war on. I wasn't staying in that hypocritical goody-goody Sweden another minute."

"Did you make a fool of yourself again?" Aunt Minna asked abruptly.

She wanted to hug him, make him welcome, tell him it didn't matter, but was that the right thing to do? This tall, bitter, bull-headed fifteen-year-old boy had gone through a lot more than she had in the two and a half years since the Germans occupied their countries. He had been in trouble already. If she was too soft with him would he endanger himself again?

Thor said tiredly, "Please put more potatoes on. I'm really hungry."

His head dropped from his hand to the table, the

sandwich slipped from his grasp. Aunt Minna looked at him with an aching, loving heart.

Karen answered the telephone.

There was a whirlpool of noise, wheezings and ghostly voices. Faintly Aunt Minna's voice came through.

"Is that Gormsgaard? May I speak to Mr. Axel, please."

"It's me, Aunt Minna," Karen shouted. "Are you coming soon?"

"Child, please, may I speak to Uncle Axel."

"He isn't home. Nor Aunt Ulrika or Grandfather Gorm. They've gone to Køge."

"In that case, try to get hold of your father. Karen, listen carefully. Tell him I'd like to consult him about a family problem. Did you get that? Remember to use the word 'consult.'" The line was fading. "Family problem."

"What is it Aunt Minna? Are you all right?"

There was only the whirlpool of noise again. Slowly Karen put the phone down. She felt empty. There was so much she wanted to tell Aunt Minna. Phone calls were no fun anymore. Even Mother was like that when calling from Copenhagen. Just when she or Kristian started to say something interesting like about the time Uncle Axel had a shipwreck on the sound with some "vacationers," she said good-by and hung up.

For a moment longer she stared out of the open window and breathed in the scent of lilac from the garden. Then she reached for the telephone, dialed the village central and gave the number of her home.

The phone rang for a long time. Even Mother wasn't there. Father never liked them calling his office, but surely this was important.

A moment later a voice she recognized came on the line. It was the voice of a reporter who used to drop in quite often, always asking a lot of questions. Mother didn't like him.

"You have a message for your father, have you, Karen?" he said pleasantly. "Let me have it."

She hadn't said anything about a message, had she? Just asked for her father. What should she do now? She could hear conversation at the other end of the line. Then a new voice spoke briskly.

"Karen? This is Uncle Borge. Do you remember me?"

"Of course I do." It was her father's friend and boss.

"Your father isn't here right now. Can you tell me what I can do for you?"

"It's Aunt Minna."

"Yes?" The voice seemed sharper.

"Our Aunt Minna from Jutland. She phoned from there. She sounded very anxious. She wanted either Uncle Axel or Father. She said it was a family problem. No, wait, she said it was important to *consult* about a family problem."

"I see. Well, don't worry, Karen. I'll see that he gets the message."

He chatted pleasantly, asking after Kristian and promising to come for a visit soon. Karen felt quite happy after the call.

She didn't see him turn to George, the reporter who had first answered the phone, and who had hung about after reluctantly relinquishing the telephone to his boss.

"Children!" the editor said lightly. "She wants Svante to bring her some books the next time he goes down to Gormsgaard. It's nice to be young and only worry about the next installment of *Anne of Green Gables.*"

Ten minutes later the editor said to his secretary, "This damned tooth. I'll have to have it out. I'll be at the dentist's for the next half an hour if anyone wants me."

George found that he had to go out too. He loitered behind his boss until he saw the editor turn in at a big office building housing a well-known dental clinic. Then he shrugged his shoulders and strolled off.

In the dental clinic the editor nodded at the receptionist. Without being announced he walked through a small office to a door marked Surgery. He knocked and the No Entrance light went off for a second. The room was fully equipped for dental work but there were no patients under care. Half a dozen men were busy writing, reading, operating a small printing press. A stack of underground papers was already bundled ready for distribution.

The editor glanced at the top sheet and grunted, "Fine. Do you know how far Svante's got on his wanderings?"

"He should be around Kalundborg by now," said the printer who, when he wasn't operating the underground press in the dental clinic, was the foreman of the pressroom of the editor's own paper.

"Can we get a message to him? His Aunt Minna wants to see him."

"That Minna is a splendid old girl. What Minna wants, Minna gets."

"It might not be anything serious, but she did use the formula, so it'll be something more than a bout of arthritis. Could be something to do with their

Norwegian family. Shipowner Eriksen's been underground for quite a time now."

"We'll get on with it."

Twenty minutes later a messenger boy left a worn suitcase packed with underground newspapers at the baggage check of the central station. A porter picked it up. The boy in a public telephone booth put in a call to Kalundborg.

An innkeeper in Kalundborg on the other side of Zealand answered the phone. He had that moment served aquavit to three Gestapo officers and he kept industriously wiping the bar as he talked.

"*Ja, ja,*" he said. "Oh, yes. The salesman was here only this morning. He didn't mention it. Thanks for the tip."

He hung up and remarked to the Germans, "It's worthwhile tipping a few contacts. Then you hear when something good is available. I like to serve only the best at my inn."

A few moments later he found a reason to go into the kitchen behind the bar. Several minutes after that his wife was hurrying down the street and seemed delighted to meet the pastor coming out of his house. The pastor was known to be absent-minded so no one wondered that he turned around and returned to his house. He was always forgetting something.

He immediately put in a call to his cousin in Århus, across the Samsø Baelt, the town where the steamer from Kalundborg landed.

His cousin, an elderly bachelor and a professor at the University of Århus, put down the phone, picked up his hat, gloves and walking stick and called his housekeeper.

"I'm going out now. I'll stop at the baker's on the way," he said.

Half an hour later the baker's boy, pushing his delivery cart in front of his bicycle, was happy to stop at the harbor. Like all the boys in the town he liked to see the steamers come in.

Svante Jensen had been glad to get on the steamer at Kalundborg. The four-hour crossing to Århus on a sunny summer's day would be relaxing. One didn't often get four hours to oneself these days.

He had found himself a nook in the bow, lit his pipe and carefully turned his back to discourage any casual conversation. The bow wave curled and broke, curled and broke, little craft went about their business in the island-spattered Baelt, gulls wheeled, the sun was hot on the top of his head and shoulders. It was almost a day out of the peaceful past.

They stopped briefly at Samsø Island, leaving a few passengers, taking on a few. He watched them embark, recognized one of them, Rolf, a man he particularly wanted to see. What luck to meet so casually, without planning.

Svante Jensen had only taken a few steps when he felt he was being watched. He glimpsed the black SS uniform out of the corner of his eye, halted to light his pipe and turned back to lean on the railing. His heart hammered. That had been close. If anything had happened, they would never have believed this had been an accidental meeting with Rolf.

The steamer had been on its way for some ten minutes when the German moved next to him and spoke. "Haven't we met before? It's Herr Jensen, isn't it?"

At least Rolf hadn't barged up, Svante Jensen thought. Now he certainly would not.

"Herr Standartenfuhrer Gruber, isn't it?" Svante Jensen said, occupying both his hands with his pipe to discourage any thought of a handshake.

"Aren't you rather far from your beat for a top Copenhagen reporter, Herr Jensen?"

"I could say the same to you, Herr Standartenfuhrer. Surely it's seldom the top brass comes to the provinces? A little vacation?"

"Is that what you are taking, Herr Jensen? Without your family? I understood you always took your family on your outings, even at night."

"This is not a vacation, unfortunately." So they had been keeping tabs on him. "Sometimes I get tired of writing only crime stories, so I get assigned to something quite different."

"Like sabotage in Jutland, perhaps?"

"I hadn't heard of that," said Svante Jensen carefully. "What's happened, or shouldn't I ask? No, I'm on the economics beat at the moment. My editor wants to have an approximation of this year's crops. I've been touring the farms."

"That should be interesting." His suspicions half-lulled, the German said, "Our controllers feel they never get quite the right figures from your farmers. As you will doubtless have better luck you will let the proper German authorities have the sum of your findings immediately on your return."

"Or advise them to take a subscription to my paper." Svante Jensen forced a grin.

The German stood needling the uneasy newspaperman for the rest of the trip. The other passengers gave them a wide berth, glaring angrily at Jensen. What was a Dane doing talking to a Gestapo officer for so long and in public? Better this way, Jensen thought; Rolf would see and wouldn't come near now.

When they landed at Århus the Gestapoman still stuck to him like a burr.

The baker's boy watched them walk together down the quay. He frowned. Then he spoke to his pals who had joined him to watch the ship come in. One of them had a ball, shouted, ran. The others skirmished after him. In a moment Svante Jensen and the Gestapoman were surrounded, then separated by wildly fighting football players, intent only on their ball, it seemed. Svante found himself edged out of the scuffle. He was thrown against the delivery wagon of the baker's boy.

"Mr. Jensen," he heard the boy say softly, "your Aunt Minna wants to see you. A consultation about a family problem.

Which was why, only several hours after telephoning Gormsgaard, Aunt Minna heard her gate creak again and looking out of the window saw her nephew Svante hurrying up the walk.

"He's asleep up in the little room under the eaves." She finished telling the story of Thor's arrival. "I'm sorry to have bothered you about such a problem, but it could have complications, I thought."

"It certainly could, and I'm glad you did. I would

have gone through the south of Jutland first and wouldn't have been here for a week at least if I hadn't received your message. Perhaps too late to prevent trouble. I must have been already on the steamer when you called Gormsgaard, so that was good going for the message. Well, at least now we know who it was. Thor!"

He laughed at Aunt Minna's puzzled face and explained, "We had a report that an unaccounted passenger had gotten off the Helsingborg-Helsingor freight-car ferry yesterday. Seemed a curious way to travel from Sweden to Denmark, stowaway, disappears on arrival, underground not alerted. We all thought the only thing we could think, that it was some sort of a German plant. Everybody's been out looking for him. Wonder why he headed here rather than Gormsgaard?"

"He's stayed with me before. I've gone to Norway at least once a year. He knows me best of the family here."

"And loves you best, as we all do. You probably haven't heard of his escapades in Norway. You'd better, so you'll know what we are in for now." Svante had another cup of Aunt Minna's home-grown sage tea and told Thor's story. She didn't ask and he didn't explain how he happened to know it so completely. .

"He appears to have done quite well in Sweden for a time, except for bothering everybody to be sent to Canada. There's a line-up of good men, better trained, more needed, ahead of him. Of course he had to wait. So up pops our young gentleman here! Now we have to get him some papers, another identity. That's all!"

"Why can't he just be my nephew come to visit?"

"Not as Thor Eriksen, son of Norwegian resistance leader Olaf Eriksen, my dear Minna. He'd be picked up and used as a hostage immediately. We heard that Olaf was captured a few weeks ago but his men got him out the same night, fortunately for him. He's a marked man. And the Germans know how to turn the screw; if they had Thor they could force Olaf to turn himself in. With young Olaf dead, Leif in the air force risking his life every day—the casualties have been up to 90 percent in the recent raids from London—Olaf would think twice of Ingeborg before sacrificing his third son. Any husband and father would. Just think about it.

"But Thor *could* be your husband's nephew, a Finnish war orphan, a Finno-Swede since he doesn't speak Finnish. The Germans can't tell the difference between Danish, Norwegian and Swedish anyhow. Yes, that might work. I'll fix it. I'll talk to Thor when he gets up. But how, dear Aunt Minna, will we keep him out of trouble?"

For a long time Aunt Minna sat, her elbows on the table, her chin in her hands, smoking her cigar. Perhaps she was remembering all the troublesome children she'd taught over the many, many years.

"Give him responsibility," she said finally.

"You could be right at that," said Svante Jensen slowly.

That evening the three of them sat around the kitchen table, talking for a long time. Svante Jensen had been out all afternoon. When he returned he had climbed to the little room under the eaves. He and Thor had had a long conversation, and the boy was subdued, but not resentful.

Now, Svante Jensen talked of Denmark. Slowly Thor began to understand the difficulties facing a country so completely different from his own Norway.

Denmark was flat farmland, Norway was mountains and forests; there had been no way to defend Denmark. Of necessity their resistance had to be less direct than the Norwegians'. Their problems were so completely different.

"The British want proof of our good will, the effectiveness of our resistance, before they'll waste valuable men and material on us. The time seems to be coming for more action. We've been doing our bit, and are doing more each day. The Allied planes had a flight route to Germany across the top of Denmark, for example, not an easy navigation job over a country completely blacked out. We had schedules for showing them the way. Many a cold winter's night your Aunt Minna here trudged up to a particular point and showed her lantern to the aircraft above. There were other Danes doing the same, making a pinprick pattern of lights for a pilot to follow. You realize, Thor, that now that you know this, Aunt Minna's life is in your hands.

"Early this week a German troop train en route to your country was blown up. Not far from here. We had a message from Norway, perhaps from your father, asking us to do it. They had learned that as well as fresh troops on board, there were some particularly adept Gestapo experts on torture. Now the Germans are going to retaliate by placing Danish hostages, anyone they happen to pick up on the street, on their trains. We'll have to blow them up just the same."

"What can I do?" Thor said.

"There will be many chances for you to help. But the first rule is, don't try to do anything without orders. Second, don't get caught. Right now lay low until I can get you your papers, which I hope will be tomorrow. There will be a house-to-house check throughout northern Jutland now."

"Because of the train explosion?"

"And because their new military airfield, which was nearly finished, unaccountably blew up."

"How do I know when I'm needed?"

"Your contact is Aunt Minna. She is very important in our organization and not many people know that. You wouldn't either, except that I suspect you'd ferret it out, staying here. Always make yourself think of her only as your aunt, a dotty old school teacher."

They laughed.

"You'll have another contact. All in good time. Don't try to find out who else is with us. Should you learn something by chance, forget it. It's safer for everybody. Now, let's try you out. Who are you? Where were you born?"

"I am Thor Jalander, called Torsti in Finland. Born in Turku. . ."

"Use Åbo, the Swedish name for Turku. You are a Swedo-Finn."

"A fine thing." For the first time Thor's old grin came back. "And me running away from Sweden."

10

Gormsgaard and Copenhagen, Denmark
AUTUMN 1942

They trudged home together in silence. Kristian slipped his hand into Karen's. She held it firmly, feeling that if he hadn't reached out, she'd have taken his. Next year she would be fifteen, but though he was one year younger, he was so tall and self-confident she seldom thought of him as her younger brother.

"We are going to tell them," he said finally.

"We'll have to, I think. You'll have a beauty of a black eye and your ear's all swollen."

"He bit it. That's when I kicked him in the stomach." His grin ended in a groan. His face was sore as a boil.

"I'm glad you did," Karen said quickly.

They came through the woods, along the path, not wanting to walk through the village. As they passed the stables they saw their father's car.

"We'd have to tell them anyhow, now," Karen said.

The twins came running to meet them, as they always did.

"Ooooh, look at Kristian! Did you win?" they shouted.

There wasn't a chance to sneak in and get cleaned up. The whole family was standing outside. Apparently the Jensens had just arrived.

Before any of the grown-ups could speak Karen said, "Holger Engst said Uncle Axel was a Nazi lover because he sold his butter and milk to them. Then he said Father was a Nazi lover too because he could always get gas for his car, so he must be doing them a lot of favors. Kristian fought him."

"But he's nearly fourteen," Aunt Ulrika cried.

Kristian tried a lopsided grin. "He looks worse than me."

"You were winning when the new teacher came and told you to stop. He could have stopped the fight earlier because I saw him watching for quite a long time."

Kristian said, "He was just snooping as usual, trying to hear if we let anything slip. He's got lots of German friends. They come to his house at night sometimes."

"You shouldn't say that—" his father looked thoughtful— "unless you are sure."

"Come on, Kristian," his mother said. "I haven't seen you for weeks but I can't kiss you through all that mud and blood."

It was that night they heard the plane going quite low over the house. They rushed out. One wing appeared to be on fire.

"It'll make Fakse Bay, I think, before it crashes. It could even pull out of the dive and make Sweden," Svante Jensen said.

"But the pilot!" Aunt Ulrika cried.

"He may have bailed out," Svante consoled her. "Axel, shall we take a little run to use up our good Nazi gas?"

The brothers exchanged an understanding look. It wasn't the first time they were going out in search of men from a British plane.

Much later, nearly at dawn, Karen and Kristian awoke because Grandfather Gorm was roaring. The grown-ups were in the drawing room and a strange pale young man was slumped in a chair.

Uncle Axel said, "Thank God this house isn't in the village or we'd all be under arrest by now. All this noise! Can't you get it into your head this country is occupied by Germans?"

"I am not occupied! I am at war," shouted Grandfather Gorm.

"Step up, man, and present yourself."

The young man stood up and limped within the range of the oil lamp. He was wearing a civilian suit but he stood at attention.

"Flight-Lieutenant Daniel Spark of the Royal Air Force, sir." He glanced at Svante and Axel Jensen and said no more.

"Glad to have you on board, sir," said Grandfather Gorm, his hand outstretched. "Aquavit! Food! Make up the guest room for the lieutenant!"

"This is much more serious than you seem to realize, Father," Uncle Axel said. "Please let me speak. I know we are all loyal Danes here but all the same I want you to think for a moment what is involved. Lieutenant Spark is in civilian clothes as you see. If the Germans capture him, he'll be shot as a spy. If they find out we have sheltered him most of us will be imprisoned, at the very least. Does everyone understand?"

"Now is as good a time as any to talk to Kristian and Karen," their mother said. "I've always wanted to take them into our confidence."

"It's only because of the danger to them," their father objected.

"When I called your office," Karen said, "I was sure that reporter who answered wasn't a good man, but I didn't know how to tell you."

"One of the people who comes to see the new schoolmaster is that Gestapoman Rudi who was here as a baby, the one Aunt Ulrika sent away," Kristian said. "I've been wanting to tell you."

"You see, Svante. They know, and they guess what they don't know."

"We were sure you and Uncle Axel only *seemed* to be cooperating with the Germans so as to find out what they were up to," Karen said.

"Are we as obvious as that, Axel?"

"It's only because we've known you well all our lives," Kristian explained, "and we love you."

Dan Spark was laughing. "What a household! I really was beginning to wonder about security when two gentlemen in a large touring car pull up casually, winkle me out of a hedge and invite me in for a drink right after we've carefully faked a plane crash. I suppose the children or some members of the family were out in a boat, saw the aircraft level off, the fire go out, and land safely in Sweden! Can we go and get my equipment now? I've hidden it, but I'm not sure whether it'll be safe in daylight."

Dan turned out to be the man the underground had been expecting, a radio operator trained by the RAF. Soon the first direct radio contact with Britain went out from the loft of Gormsgaard stables.

A week later Dan rode to Copenhagen in the trunk of the car and came back by train, openly, with a new identity. The village heard that he was a reporter friend of Svante Jensen's who had been covering the war and needed a rest. That explained why he took sea air in the dune cottage of Kristian's friend, Mrs. Knudsen, the writer. Later he stayed with other friends of the Jensens as well. It wasn't safe to send radio messages from the same place all of the time.

Karen and Kristian didn't know at the time what sort of messages he sent, but sometimes they helped to pass them on to him. It started by accident.

Kristian was bicycling home one evening when close to the gate of their drive a boy he had never seen before spoke to him.

"My tire's flat and my pump won't work."

"Try mine."

The boy glanced up and down the road. There was only a farmer's car going away from them.

"Your name's Kristian Jensen, isn't it?" The boy was pretending to pump his wheel. The pump seemed all right to Kristian.

"Yes, it is. Why?"

"Just put my pump on your bike and go home. Give it to your father."

"But you said it's no good," Kristian objected. "You give my pump back after you've fixed your wheel."

"Go. Go now, someone's coming." The boy

looked up with very blue, very frightened eyes. They could both hear a car beyond the bend.

Kristian got on his bike, turned up his own drive and kept going though he heard the car stop and German voices shouting at the boy.

His father wasn't at Gormsgaard but he knew it was all right to consult Uncle Axel. He watched his uncle unscrew the pump, pull out a piece of paper and quickly put it back inside.

"That's for Dan. It's marked urgent. I can't take it. I've no reason to go to the fishing village tonight."

"I'll take it," Kristian said. "I'll get my fishing rod and creel and I'll fish from the wharf for a time. Then I'll go to Mrs. Knudson's to get warm. I often do. How about that?"

"Your father wouldn't like it. He knows the dangers all too well."

"But Mother would say everything we do for the Allies counts toward Denmark's freedom and honor."

After that, when Karen was shopping in one or the other of the villages near to them, quite often the woman behind the counter would hand her the sales slip and make a point of saying, "Don't lose that now. Your aunt will want to check the prices."

It would turn out to be something in code and quite inscrutable.

Nina and Torsten found out. They had come to visit the day Karen had brought home a message and Kristian was going to go off on a fishing expedition to take it to Dan Spark.

"You cannot go, Kristian. You've been there already three times this week," they heard Uncle Axel say. "It's entirely too risky."

"How about me?" Torsten said from the doorway. Uncle Axel nearly dropped with shock. "I guessed something was up because Kristian wouldn't let me go with him."

"If you were caught it would be even worse for you than for Kristian."

"I'm a Dane too," Torsten said.

The woman writer in the dunes cottage always had lots of children visiting her. She wrote children's books and liked children. So now no one thought it odd to see them come and go at her house. Dan stayed there more and more—it was safer than Gormsgaard. With Torsten and Nina helping, no one had to make more than one trip a week to the cottage.

One day a gentleman Karen had never met stopped her on the street, sent greetings to Uncle Axel and shook her hand. When he had strolled away, she looked. He had left a note in her palm.

"Everybody is shaking hands all over Denmark

these days, even more than before, particularly in crowded city streets," her father remarked with a laugh when she told him. "But very few get the sort of message you've just brought home. This particular one must go to Dan. It may be just a joke about the Germans, or a rude song about them, or sometimes an item from a British broadcast the Germans wouldn't want us to know."

Finally the young people felt they were really helping Denmark's fight for freedom.

Pelle and Lotte were growing fast. They were almost five. While there were food shortages all over Denmark now, with the Germans seizing everything they could lay their hands on to send back to Germany, it wasn't so bad on a farm. You could grow your own grain, vegetables and fruit, and hide some when the German inspectors came to check on your crops. You could also try to hide some of your chickens, geese and pigs, and lie about how much cattle you had slaughtered for meat. And there was still fish in the sea.

The twins got the best of everything of course. They needed it most. They didn't remember such luxuries as oranges and bananas, real chocolate and real cake, and what the grown-ups missed the most, real coffee and tea, they wouldn't have had anyhow.

They were wild and happy and got under everyone's feet. They loved Aunt Ulrika and everyone else too, and appeared to remember their mother and father only in their prayers each night.

"I think the twins need to know there is a world outside Gormsgaard," said Uncle Axel one day. "Karen and Kristian, what do you think, shall we take them to Copenhagen for the king's birthday?"

"Can we go! As we did before the Germans came?" Karen was delighted. "And he'll come on the balcony and we'll shout, '*Konge, Konge, Konge, Kom nu frem, ellers Gaar vi aldrig hjem*' (King, king, king, out you come, or we'll never go home)."

"It may be a little different this year. We shall see."

It was completely different.

It wasn't during daylight as it used to be, with people laughing, shouting and singing and carrying flowers. The celebration was planned for the evening.

Despite the curfew they left home in the late dusk. Svante Jensen had handed everyone a lantern, tiny ones for the twins.

Out in the streets of Copenhagen there were already many people. By the time they got to Kongens

129

Nytor Square people were coming from all directions. On the broad Bredgade they walked four and five abreast.

There was no pushing even when they turned into the narrow streets leading to the Royal Palace of Amalienborg. Four streets led into the large octagonal courtyard enclosed by the four wings of the palace.

It had been a good idea to leave when they did because at least they were quite close now. Masses of people soon blocked the four entrances to the square. Someone behind them murmured that in his suburb the Germans had tried to stop people and arrest them for breaking curfew. More Danes immediately joined up until they were ten times stronger than the German patrol. There wasn't anything the Germans could do.

As it grew darker Svante Jensen lighted the blackout lanterns. The light was only a tiny blue flame, but one by one, dozen by dozen, hundred by hundred, the firefly lights went on. The singing began softly and grew and echoed mutedly against the palace walls, rose and sounded over the blacked-out city.

Far back a door opened on the balcony they all knew. The thin, tall, familiar figure came out. He too was carrying a lantern with a tiny flickering flame.

He stood there a long time, straight and kingly. They sang to him.

Finally he lifted his hand. The silence spread into the streets where the people couldn't see their king.

"Thank you, thank you," he said softly, slowly. Those who were closest whispered his words to those behind them. The pervading whisper linked them all as one family. "Thank you, thank you. Go home now, quietly. God bless you. Good night."

11

Jutland, Denmark
SPRING 1943

If Thor leaned backward out of the little window of his room under the eaves, gripping the window seat with his knees and hanging on firmly to the top of the window frame, he could see only the sky and the clouds above him. Sometimes he saw planes high and far. Then for a moment he would be the pilot, zooming up to shoot German aircraft with the black swastika on their wings, bringing them down before they could reach Norway.

Sitting on his windowsill this morning he thought of Leif somewhere in the northern Canadian woods, by a wilderness lake at a settlement of log barracks called Vesle Skaugum. Uncle Svante had produced a letter from his mother at Christmas time which gave the news. Actually, by now Leif might be the pilot of one of the planes that flew across at night and dropped supplies to the Danish Resistance. Or he could be fighting air battles over London or the English Channel, or Egypt, or even dropping bombs on Germany. Leif's letter had taken a long time to get to Norway and his mother's message to Thor had traveled by a slow subterranean route: snowy mountains, slow Sweden, frozen straits. The second half of the good news was that his father was still free and carrying on in the Norwegian Resistance.

Thor was proud of them. He was almost happy himself. He had had a lot to do. Every week there were more chores for him.

First he had only delivered the underground paper, each week on different days, at different times, to different places. He had needed a new bicycle, but Aunt Minna had pointed out that an old rusty one was better camouflage. When at last he got one new tire from a lot dropped by an RAF plane, he had taken care to scrape and stain it, to make it look old. The Germans had eyes everywhere.

When the underground began to print books which were prohibited by the Germans, he had gotten a chance to take some of them around. This was trickier because they were bulkier than the news sheets. There had to be a system to everything, and every time one went out of one's own door there had to be a good reason for being on the road *besides* the real one.

The first time a German patrol had stopped him

he was so scared he was ready to fight. Push them, pummel them, run. The hardest thing he'd ever done, he told Aunt Minna later, was to shuffle his feet, grin, act stupid but polite, as Uncle Svante had advised. Now he even said hello to some of the local German patrols, wishing he didn't have to, but that was part of his act.

Who was to know that in the little white cottage with its red window shutters and green slate roof in the countryside near Århus Thor each day did stiffer lessons set for him by Aunt Minna than he would have done in any school. After his last examination they had figured out that he was at least a whole year ahead of his normal peacetime class. The lessons seemed easier now because he wanted to work.

One wintry night Thor was in bed when he heard muffled conversation downstairs. Aunt Minna opened a door and called him. She was talking as she came down the stairs. "He is a dependable boy. You can trust him."

He recognized the man in the kitchen, a hotel owner from the nearest town. There were no introductions.

"We are a man short for a job. If you'll lend us a hand will you promise to forget the people, the place and the occasion afterward?"

"Yes," Thor said. "I'll get ready."

A few days later a new German factory was blown up. Thor knew that the supplies for the job had arrived the night he had helped the hotel owner to signal a plane, for he had also helped to gather the cases while the men in the shadows speedily got them away to various hiding places. He had been scared, of course, but there was a good feeling in doing something useful.

After that night Thor found himself carrying messages. Most of the time he didn't know where they came from and he was careful not to try to find out where they were ultimately going.

His Uncle Svante had explained to him the importance of cutouts. In the underground press, for example, journalists, printers, packers and distributors were strictly unknown to one another. Should there be a betrayal or a random raid, the unfortunate captives would have nothing to tell about the rest. Newspaper copy would go from the reporter by courier to a cutout on the street, in a park, at a station, who handed it to only one other person whom he might never meet again. "You are a cutout, Thor," Uncle Svante had said. "A sort of safety valve for many."

All the same, inevitably he began to know and recognize many of the loyal Danes in the countryside and the villages who risked capture, prison and possible torture in going about their self-imposed tasks. He never stopped to think that the same thing applied to him.

He came home one spring evening from his underground paper route to find Aunt Minna boiling beetroot and potatoes. A jar of home-pickled herring and a loaf of rye bread were already on the table. Aunt Minna was talking to herself as usual. Smiling, he stopped to listen.

". . . and if he's caught they'll make him talk. If he tries to run away he'll be shot. But Henning said there was no one else. The pastor shot, the Hansen boys sent to Germany, Harald in prison, Jorge God knows where. All on the same day! Betrayed. We must find the traitor."

"What is it I must do, Aunt Minna?" Thor was no longer smiling.

The old woman dropped into a chair and stared at him blankly.

"As Henning says, *it could be one of us.* Until we find the informer we cannot trust anyone who has had access to our group."

Thor put his arms around Aunt Minna. "Shall I make limeflower or acorn?"

"Coffee might help, even out of acorns. That limeflower tea I find a bit too much. If anything happens to you, my Thor, I will never be able to face your mother."

"She'll understand. My father would not expect less from me than from my brothers. What about this informer?"

She pulled herself together with an effort and talked to Thor as an adult. "There is only you. I cannot go. Henning cannot go. We may already be suspected. We couldn't possibly leave unnoticed. The information is vital. It must get to Aalborg . . ."

That same evening Thor bicycled to Århus. He left his bike at a baker's shop where Aunt Minna was a customer. He hung about the harbor until he found a truck heading north, and got himself a lift. Unfortunately it was going only as far as Randers, but on their way they had seen a train chugging north, so he made his way to the station.

There were a lot of Germans, soldiers and Gestapo around but he thought he would chance it. It was a troop train, but there were a number of freight cars tagged on to the end of it. Thor stuck to the shadows, didn't hurry and kept his face vacant-looking, his mouth open. If a beam from a guard's flashlight happened to catch him, he wanted to look stupid.

It had begun to drizzle when they reached Aalborg. In the murk Thor slipped away, bypassing the station, climbing a fence, skirting a field. He knew he had to take himself to Budolfi Plads, the old part of the town. Aunt Minna had drawn him a map which he had studied before they burned it. What with sailing and many climbs in the mountains, he had a good sense of direction.

The doorway was three stone steps up from the street. He felt the knocker with his fingers. It was the shape of a sea horse, which was as it should be. He knocked three times, then twice. He waited a long time, then knocked again.

Finally a frightened, wrinkled old face under a white nightcap peered through the crack of the door.

"Dr. Klaus," Thor said. "I have a message for Dr. Klaus."

"He isn't here."

"Where is he?"

The door was closing. He put his foot in the crack. Only in an emergency was he to use his aunt's name. This old woman couldn't possibly be with the Germans. He felt sure of it.

"I'm from Minna of Gormsgaard," he said. "I *must* see the doctor."

"Come in, boy."

They stood in the dimly lit hall. The old woman lifted her oil lamp so the light fell on his face.

"Hmmm." She stared at him. "There's a bit of

Old Axel of Gormsgaard about you. When he was wild and young. Yes, so there is. All the same, Dr. Klaus is not here. Gone to Copenhagen. Not taken, they wouldn't dare. Just gone for an interview."

"What'll I *do?*" Thor felt desperate. "This is important."

"Come. I'll heat the soup. Good soup. Won't do you any harm."

She watched him all the time he ate but Thor didn't mind. He was cold, hungry and desperate. The soup eased the first two, but the problem remained. What was he to do now?

"There's a street with three undertakers on it," the old woman was saying slowly. "If you go to the back door of the middle one, knock as you did here and ask for Master Carpenter Lyngby. He might be able to help you. I've taken messages there for the doctor."

Absently she added, "Many a good boy has left there in a coffin."

"What!"

She filled his soup bowl again, buttered another slice of bread and cut a big slab of cheese. She cackled, "Alive, boy, alive. The Germans aren't going to open every coffin they see."

Thor let out his breath. She obviously thought he was on the run. Good. Svante Jensen had said that it was better if even your best friend didn't know what you were doing. Always muddy your tracks.

She gave him directions in her rambling way. After half an hour he thought he was lost. An hour later he knew he was.

It was sure to be here somewhere! Perhaps the shop windows were shuttered so he couldn't see the coffins. She had said they were white. He stumbled against a low stone wall, sat there in the drizzly dark and tried to concentrate.

The attack came from behind. Arms around his neck, his waist, his feet. Like an octopus. He tried to shake himself free, swore, and heard gasped words in Danish.

"What do you think you are doing?" he hissed.

"We want to know what you are up to, chum."

"Who are you?"

"The Churchill Club."

"The what?"

"We fight for freedom." It was a boy's voice.

An even younger one said, "We are in jail all day long for what we did. But they can't keep us chained."

"Don't babble, you idiots." It was a squeaky command.

"If you are in jail all day long, what are you doing here?"

Thor was sure these were just boys. No danger here unless they made too much noise. The thought came to him like a shock that they were just like he had been, making a game of war, getting in the way.

"We found a way to escape."

"Every night we go out and do some sabotage."

"We go back before anyone notices we are gone, and all day we sit in the prison like good boys and do our lessons." The first voice had a chuckle in it.

"We are in a Danish police jail, not German. Our fathers made sure of that."

"Stop, you idiots," ordered the third boy. "How do you know who he is."

"I'm on a serious job myself. It's urgent, important for Denmark," Thor said. "You can help me. Tell me how to get to a street with three undertaker shops."

"We know that!" said the three boys and led the way.

There was no difficulty after that. In the carpentry shop behind the back door of the middle undertaker's he was questioned by a tall white-haired man who was Master Carpenter Lyngby. He seemed to have been expecting the message Thor dug out of the lining of his cap.

"Good boy. We can act on this immediately. If you hadn't managed to get here tonight, good men might have been lost, a splendid opportunity certainly missed. Wait here."

He went through a side door and Thor heard a mumble of voices. The master carpenter came back looking pleased.

"I want you to tell your Aunt Minna we'll also help with the problem in her district. She is not to worry, we may have a lead already. I won't have time to organize your return trip. I have to get on with the information you brought. Can you manage?"

"Yes, sir," Thor said, "if I don't meet those little kids again."

He explained. Master Lyngby smiled wryly. "Their intentions are good but they are asking for trouble for everybody. I realize it's different in your Norway, as it is in poor brave Poland, where anything at all done against the Germans is a step forward and no one can be worse off than they are already. Here we are just starting to fight back. We live in such an open country we must take more care. Some little mosquitoes molesting the enemy can lead them to people who are in the resistance. Try to steer clear of them."

"Who are they, sir?"

"Schoolboys. Patriotic schoolboys. They formed a Churchill Club, they sang forbidden songs, wore RAF colors and then started on their brand of sabotage to annoy the Germans. The Gestapo picked them up, but our own police, with some help from Copenhagen, managed to get them jailed in a Danish prison, out of harm's way. So now they are out again."

"I did the same sort of thing myself," Thor said, swallowing, "at home in Norway. Some brave men may have been captured, shot, because of me."

"We all try to do our best," Master Carpenter Lyngby said, and shook hands firmly with Thor.

Thor had barely turned the corner to the next narrow street, thinking he'd try for a lift in a truck on the outskirts of town, when the octopus of young arms grabbed him again. They pulled him to the ground.

"It's your turn to tell us who you are!"

"Are you really on a big job?"

"We can help, you know."

Thor could see them now. The rain had stopped, the sky was becoming lighter. There were three smallish boys about twelve or thirteen.

"Isn't it time for you to get back to your jail?" He tried to keep anger out of his voice. "Can't you see it's dawn. Beat it."

He shook himself free and sprinted off. The boys ran after him, forgetting in their excitement to be quiet. He turned the corner and skidded to a stop. He held his arms wide to block the rush of the others.

"You morons, now see what you've done!"

They had emerged into a little square. From the far end a patrol-car engine roared. The lights blazed, catching Thor fully in their glare.

"Run!" He gave a sharp shove to the small boys behind him. "That way! I'll try to lead them off."

A lane too narrow for a car led to the right. The small boys scuttled down it. Thor sprinted up the street. Surely there was another lane. As the mudguards of the patrol car scraped him he found it, jumped left into its narrow safety and ran.

The shouting was behind him, around him, ahead of him. He didn't know where he was going, but at least he was leading the pursuit away from those foolish kids. The lane ended in a wide street.

A car was parked across the foot of the lane.

His way was blocked!

In a doorway flush to the street there was a thin wedge of shadow. The rain that had been a drizzle beat down harder. The patrol appeared to decide not to get wet. No one left the car.

Thor tried to catch his breath. What had he almost remembered? Something helpful? A way to safety?

He had it! The old woman, telling him where to go, had said, ". . . many a good boy has left there in a coffin . . ."

Lyngby might not have time to help him on his return trip, but surely he'd have no objection if Thor had a little rest in one of his coffins.

He made certain there was no longer any sign of the small boys. Then, sticking to the shadows, he made his way back up the street.

It took him a day and a half to get back to Aunt Minna's, hitchhiking when he thought it seemed safe, hiking cross country, borrowing bicycles when he could.

Aunt Minna hugged him hard.

"Thank God," she said, and added briskly, "get your things together."

"Are we going somewhere?"

"We are, and as quickly as possible. I was only waiting for you to get back. They have been at me to leave, but I knew you'd make your way here."

"Has something happened?" Thor asked.

"Something will happen if we don't get away quickly. I've been warned."

"I won't take long," Thor said. He didn't have much to pack, after all.

An hour later he heaved their cases into Aunt Minna's old car while she locked up her little house.

They drove through Odense where Hans Christian

Andersen used to live, caught the ferry from Nyborg to Korsor and then on to Ringsted. There Aunt Minna left the main roads for the narrow country lanes twisting by fields and copses toward the sound. But Thor saw nothing of the spring-green sights. He slept his way across Denmark.

He woke up only as the car turned onto the long gravel drive. The geese and swans were swimming in the pond, as always. Then there was the gentle old house and Karen, running down the steps.

It was nearly four years to the day since he had last been to Gormsgaard.

12

Gormsgaard, Denmark
SUMMER 1943

Here it was a different world.

Thor swung in the hammock, smelled the lilacs, the freshly mowed grass. The birds sang in the orchard, bees hummed in the flower garden, an indignant duck led her family of ducklings from the swan pond to the pool in the woods. The two remaining peacocks strutted and fanned their tails. People in peril, countries at war, as all over Europe, seemed far from the little world of Gormsgaard this morning.

Thor looked at Karen crossing the lawn and wondered if this slender girl with long silvery-blond hair could possibly be the little burrlike girl cousin he remembered—the one who had given him the flowers for luck. He had been thinking of that ever since he had arrived with Aunt Minna at Gormsgaard.

Karen was thinking how different the tall thin boy with hollow cheeks and so very serious dark eyes was from the bumptious Thor she remembered. Only the thick shock of dark hair and the long dark eyelashes were the same.

Kristian joined them, carefully carrying a tray, the twins bouncing around him. He put it on the garden table and stirred the contents of a big jug.

"If autumn doesn't come soon we'll be out of apple juice. Even this isn't too good, cousin Thor, because we had to pick most of the apples before they were ripe; otherwise the Others would have found a way to get them. There was no sugar either, but Aunt Ulrika's become a criminal and hid most of our honey."

"We know what 'the Others' means," said one of the twins.

"It means 'nasty Germans,'" said the other twin.

"Hush," said Karen.

"You remember the game," Kristian said. "Not a single German can make you say one word. Come along, we'll practice while we feed the ducks."

Thor sat up. The morning's complete peace was cracked.

"Is that necessary?"

"Yes," Karen nodded. "They babble so, the twins. We lost half a dozen geese which we'd taken to the

pool at the back of the farm when we were warned
the Germans were coming to do their inventory. The
twins told them everything about the 'nice geese
babies, come and see.' So Kristian invented the
game."

"Does it work?"

"It has, up to now. We hope they'll remember it
if anything serious happens. They're half Jewish, you
know."

"Surely the Germans won't get away with their
tricks here in Denmark," Thor said. During his
months in Jutland he had come to realize that Denmark was fighting the enemy in her own way.

Before Karen could answer, Kristian called her.
He was on his bicycle and leading hers.

"Keep an eye on the little kids, Thor," he waved.
"Aunt Ulrika will collect them in a minute!"

Thor swung in the hammock a little longer, thinking. Where were his cousins off to again? On the
surface everything here at Gormsgaard seemed fine,
but everyone had a habit of disappearing at odd
hours.

At odd hours! That was it. They must be doing
the same sort of chores he had done in Jutland, and
here he was, just taking it easy.

But whom should he talk to, report to for duty?
Grandfather Gorm?

He met his Aunt Ulrika in the hall.

"I suspect," he said directly, "that everyone is busy doing underground chores in this household. I'm on my way to ask Grandfather Gorm what I can do."

"Your Uncle Svante *thought* a week or so was all you could take of inactivity. He's just phoned, he'll be coming tonight. Wait and talk to him. Please, don't speak of resistance or underground work to your grandfather. He won't keep it to himself. He believes in shouting his beliefs out loud and fighting face to face like Vikings!"

"What a splendid old man he is," Thor said.

"Yes," Aunt Ulrika said with a sigh, "but it can be dangerous."

Svante Jensen came that evening. When he and Thor found themselves alone in the stables he said, "Can you drive a car, Thor?"

"Not well," said Thor, remembering the day in Lillehammer.

"I'll speak to Axel. Perhaps you can practice a short time each day in the back lanes. It may be useful one of these days. Meanwhile, just hold your horses, there'll be lots to do. Soon enough, I'm afraid."

In August the rumor went around that the Germans were going to disarm the Danish army, perhaps dismiss the Danish police. More people were arrested and imprisoned for small incidents like speaking to German soldiers in English, or shouting at them when they marched by. The workers went on strike in the shipyards, and in sympathy people stopped working in factories, shops and offices. The Danes were getting fed up with their government's do-nothing policy, there were serious food shortages, and the Germans were at last being defeated. They had been thrown back in Russia and in North Africa, Sicily had been invaded, Mussolini overthrown.

Svante Jensen pointed out to Thor that while in July there had been 84 acts of sabotage, in August there were 198. And a good thing too, he said.

"If we don't act ourselves, the British will take the initiative. When they bombed the biggest factory in Copenhagen in January, a lot of Danes were killed. We could have sabotaged it ourselves, warned all Danish workers, but there were just not enough of us to do the job. There was a message from the Allies—either we fight here ourselves or we take our chances when they bomb us. It's reasonable."

There were new ultimatums, prohibitions on public gatherings and stricter curfews; all firearms had to be handed in and there were bans on everything. The cabinet resigned and the Parliament dissolved itself to disassociate themselves from working with the Germans. The king declared himself a prisoner of war as a sign of protest against the invasion. All the ships in Copenhagen Navy Yard were scuttled by their Danish crews. Censorship of the press united all the newspapermen. The underground papers got better, reported all the news and came out regularly.

But at Gormsgaard the summer days were still long, warm and peaceful. The fruit ripened on the trees.

Thor fretted for action.

"Thor," she called. "Is there a car you can use? Please go immediately and get Dr. Holstein. Make certain his whole family comes as well. And try to get hold of Uncle Axel. No, not through here, try the telephone at the village post office. Just say there's 'a consultation about a family problem.'"

Thor's face had gone pale. He was staring at the people in the car as though he had seen ghosts.

"In Norway I saw the trains leaving for Germany." His voice was shaky. "Packed with Norwegian prisoners."

"And don't talk to anyone about anything," Mai Jensen snapped in a voice quite unlike her. "Come right back."

"It won't be . . . like in Norway . . . here?"

"It will not. Don't think of it. Hurry."

"What's he talking about?" Karen was still on the running board.

"Your father will be here soon, my child. He'll explain."

But there were no explanations when Svante Jensen drove up less than half an hour later. His car too was loaded with people, some of whom Karen thought she recognized. Her mother was hurrying her away.

"Run to help Aunt Ulrika and Aunt Minna." She turned to two young men who had come with her husband. "Go with my daughter, please. I think we had better put up some trestle tables in the old kitchen, the way we do for harvest festivals. She'll show you."

"And beds?" asked Karen slowly, puzzled.

"First of all get some good long linen tablecloths. The best ones. Then see if you can help the mothers with the small children. Check that there is enough hot water, soap and towels. Or look after the other children, show them the bathroom, your old toys."

Her mother sounded frantic; she usually made sense. She couldn't do *all* of those things at *once*. She would look for Aunt Minna.

"But who *is* everybody?" Karen had to know. "Why are they all so quiet!"

"Later, darling. Later."

Axel Jensen had met Thor halfway to the village, come home, had a talk with his brother and driven away again.

Meanwhile a Copenhagen taxicab drove up and brought another half a dozen people. Karen counted in her head that now there must be at least twenty-six adults, six children and four babies. Then she lost count because two more cars, driven by friends of her parents turned up.

In the big old kitchen that was part of the stables, the cook was blessing herself for having baked that day, and now she was making fish soup and boiling chickens and vegetables. Svante Jensen moved quickly through the groups of men, introducing them to one another when they were strangers, speaking cheerfully, firmly. "Don't worry, don't worry," Karen heard him say again and again. "We'll do the best we can."

Thor came back with the Holsteins. The pastor from the village drove up in his horse and cart. Aunt Ulrika was asking everyone to come to the long old kitchen, the beams glowing by lantern and candle-light.

That was when Grandfather Gorm stomped out of the main house, tall, old, white-haired, leaning on his stick and shouting, "What's it all about? What's happening! Why am I not told anything?"

"Thor, Kristian, get his chair from the dining room," Aunt Minna said quickly. "Axel, Svante, you cannot keep your father out of this now."

His two sons went to the old man. They talked to him earnestly. He seemed to crumble.

"Not in Denmark. God of our fathers, not in Denmark!" he said.

Then with great dignity he walked through the throng of his unexpected guests, shaking hands, say-ing in a low, shaky voice, "Welcome to Gormsgaard. You are welcome to Gormsgaard."

When the many silent, strangely silent, guests and the family were at last seated at the tables, oddly festive with the best linen and silver, with delicious-smelling food so hastily made, Karen thought she would cry. She did not know why, but she felt like crying.

Uncle Axel stood up.

He usually looked very elegant, as though he combed his hair every few minutes and had his coat pressed twice a day. His face was gray now, and there were tired lines on his forehead, beneath his eyes, around the corners of his mouth. He had met bravery and treachery, understanding and coldness that day, but he couldn't tell about that. Since his younger brother had telephoned him, he had tried to do his job at the creamery and still organize people who were for goodness and for freedom. Though he had helped the Resistance, he had taken a pleasant life for granted. He never would again.

"With my father I say welcome to Gormsgaard," he said. "Thank you for trusting us and coming so quickly. My brother knows more about what has happened in our Denmark today. I'll let him tell us about it."

Svante Jensen found it difficult to start. He looked down at the long tables and into the eyes of the grim-looking men, the frightened women. Even the young people and children seemed to ask him to say this was not true. But it was true, and he would have to say it. Better briefly and bluntly.

"Today we know for a fact that the Germans intend to round up all the Danish Jews. Their ships are already coming into Copenhagen harbor to take you away to their concentration camps.

"We suspected they were not going to keep their promise to leave us, all of us—Danes of whatever faith—in peace. On the seventeenth of September, they raided the Jewish Community Center. They went there in civilian clothes, thieves in the night. They stole your records of all the names and addresses of Danish Jews. We heard about it, and it was obvious to everyone who thought clearly that every one of our Jewish compatriots was now in danger.

"The foreign minister, Niels Svenningsen, was advised. He called upon Werner Best, the German administrative officer in Denmark. When he lodged his protest at this outrage against Danish citizens he was told that it was 'nothing at all, nothing at all.' He knew it wasn't only '*Eine recht kleine Aktion*,' a mere small action, looking for saboteurs, because we have always known who are the saboteurs and who are not in Denmark. So we reported this act to C. B. Henriques, the head of the Jewish community. We have also told him today what has happened. He refuses to believe it. He believes more in Denmark's power to save our own citizens than we do. I am sorry he is in the wrong. The Germans *are* ready to act.

"We have no arms, no fighting power. All we can do is to try to get you away. You are, as we are, Danish. Germans have an evil power. We cannot save you in any other way except to send you away from your own—our own—homeland.

"Today two German transport vessels are arriving in Copenhagen harbor. We don't want one of our friends, one of our fellow citizens, to be on those boats."

Around the tables there was a sigh like a storm wind rising in the forest. It was a sigh of deep sorrow. Then there was a sound of crying.

"But they will not succeed!" Grandfather Gorm banged on the table. "You are safe already! You are here."

Svante Jensen continued, "Tonight is the night before your Rosh Hashanah Eve, the beginning of your New Year festivities. Tomorrow, the Germans think, all of you will be at your synagogues or in your homes. That's why they picked this time to arrest you. They thought they would find every one of you since they have your names and addresses."

"There are at least eight thousand Danish Jews," said Dr. Holstein very slowly.

"One cannot save eight thousand of one's countrymen in one minute," Svante Jensen snapped. "As soon as we were certain of the dreadful truth my family, and people like my family, began to go to every Jewish friend we had. All day tomorrow other Danes will go and warn their friends."

"Some of us thought we were Germans too once," said a man who had escaped from Germany, a brother of a friend of the Jensens.

"And Poles! And look what happened to the Jews of Norway!"

"And Belgium! Holland! All over the world!"

"You are *Danes,*" roared Grandfather Gorm, his loud voice echoing from the beams. "Would you let *us* suffer!"

"Why should Christians stand by Jews?" a voice said.

The man next to him at the table said furiously, "And when have the Jews ever helped themselves? In all history?"

"But where can we go? You can't keep us here until the end of the war." It was the mother of four children. "They'll find us, if not tomorrow, the day after tomorrow. And what will happen to you then for sheltering us?"

"You are not staying here," Svante Jensen raised his voice. "You are going to Sweden. My brother has been arranging for boats to take you all. Before dawn tomorrow you will be in safety and freedom. And tomorrow many more will join you, many more Danes of your faith."

"But will the Swedes let us land on their shores?"

"It has been arranged," Axel Jensen said sharply. He didn't add that he remembered what a stiff piece of negotiation that had been, and how many people had helped. Or perhaps one would say a few. A few brave ones.

The old woman who had come in Aunt Minna's car put her arms around her grandchildren and said, "Why have we been chosen out of so many—so many in danger?"

"Because we knew you. You were the easiest to reach immediately, quickly," Svante Jensen said. "Your son is my wine merchant. My wife shops with the Eljsbergs. Not everyone would believe an acquaintance who comes to you and says, pack only a small bag, leave your arrangements for your New Year's festivities, come with us. We started with you because there are almost eight thousand more Danes of your faith whom we must reach before tomorrow night. Please write down the names of all your friends and acquaintances and they will be warned and helped. Karen, please get some paper and pencils."

The pastor of the village turned to Grandfather Gorm. "I am not of the faith of our guests but the same God looks after us all. Shall I say grace?"

"Say grace, say grace," Grandfather Gorm said. "Good warm soup will not hurt anyone at this moment."

It was a strange September party that night before New Year's Eve. Karen would remember the old huge kitchen, the candles fluttering, the lanterns low, and how much stranger it must have seemed to these friends of her parents going away from their homes. Yet somehow, after her father had made his terrible, sad speech, everyone seemed easier. There were questions and arguments. Several people even said it must all be a mistake.

That's when Dr. Holstein had his say.

"Half of you know me. I have been your doctor, but I thought I could run away by leaving Copenhagen. I realize no one can escape this present terror. I have talked with our chief rabbi, and he is as convinced as I am that our Danish friends are telling us the truth. We must thank God we have such friends. Friends who risk their lives to help us."

Svante Jensen said, "I've been hoping you would go with this first group. You could be of tremendous help to our Danish compatriots in Sweden."

Dr. Holstein shook his head slowly. "I may be of

more help here, Svante. I am a doctor after all. I'd like to see that most of my people get away before I go, if I must go."

He nodded at a big fair man. "Nils Bergman, you are a lawyer, are you not? I have met you at the synagogue."

"So he is," Svante Jensen said with relief. "Please, Nils, let me tell you everything I know about the arrangements in Sweden."

"*After* dinner," said Aunt Minna. There were tears in her eyes. "When you all come home again we will have a better feast of Rosh Hashanah."

"Here at Gormsgaard," bellowed Grandfather Gorm, "I expect everyone of you back home here at Gormsgaard. I'll live until then. See if I don't."

14

Gormsgaard and Copenhagen, Denmark
SEPTEMBER 30, 1943

Everyone at Gormsgaard was up by dawn that September 30. No unexpected visitor would have found a trace of the crowd of guests who had been there the night before. The big kettles, pots and pans hung shining from their usual hooks in the old kitchen. The guest rooms looked unused for weeks. The boys had raked the gravel on the walks and by the stables. Any extra rubbish had already been burned.

Despite the dangers of the day ahead, the folk of Gormsgaard were cheerful.

A telephone call had come from Sweden. The voice had been that of a pleasant-sounding woman who asked for Aunt Ulrika as though she was an old friend and gossiped with her for a time. She also happened to mention that her husband and sons had been fishing all night.

"All the catch was landed safely, every—ah fish," she said with a chuckle. "We *like*—ah, fish."

"That's one woman I'd like to meet after the war," Aunt Ulrika said, her eyes streaming with tears as she hung up the phone.

In the early morning Axel and Svante Jensen and Dr. Holstein locked themselves into the library for consultation. When they came out for breakfast they looked alert despite the lack of sleep they shared with everyone else. Aunt Ulrika, who had hidden honey from the Germans, made them a creamy coffee from what was left of the real coffee. Today everyone would need all their strength, all their energy.

Svante Jensen, though he was the younger brother, was now in charge. He had been, since the first days of the occupation, in the small Danish group who wanted to fight and not give in.

"Everyone ready then?" he asked. "Aunt Minna has already gone to her job." She will not be in Copenhagen but Kristian, Thor, Torsten, I want you to listen to me carefully. What I ask you to do today is dangerous. Most dangerous of all to Torsten, but his father asked me not to leave him out of the plan. You must say, honestly, whether you want to come or not."

"What about *me!*" Karen said.

"We're coming, of course," the boys said it in the same breath and turned to grin at one another.

Svante Jensen said, "Boys on bicycles is the most natural sight in all of Denmark. You will come with me to Copenhagen and you will be the messengers. Torsten, as his father says, will be useful in convincing people they must leave quickly—today—because a lot of them know him as the son of Dr. Holstein."

He turned to his wife. "Mai, you will please help Axel. All day he will be trying to round up transportation. At the same time he must appear in his office, go through his usual routine, because the Germans may be watching him. We have to be extremely careful but we must try to round up every fisherman's boat, every motorboat, every yacht on our part of the coast. You have a sharp instinct about good people and bad people. Many fishermen will want to be paid, but that doesn't necessarily make them bad. But use your judgment before you tell anyone why we want boats tonight."

"And me?" Karen asked again.

Aunt Ulrika said, "And me?"

"Someone has to stay at home. To take messages. They may not sound reasonable but try to understand them. I can't say very often that there are six more loaves of bread on the way, and I cannot say that we will have so many more guests over and over again. There may be many strangers coming to the house by taxi, walking from the bus and railway stations, driven by people unknown to you. Mrs. Holstein will stay here to make certain someone who could betray everyone is not among these people. Karen, you'll just have to stay here and help your Aunt Ulrika and Mrs. Holstein. You'll see. There will be emergencies."

"Why should you do this for us, for my people?" Mrs. Holstein's voice was close to tears.

"For goodness sake, Judith," Svante Jensen said impatiently, "this house is conveniently close to the coast and Axel knows a lot of people with boats! Come along, boys."

Already at that early hour the newspaper office was busy. Listening to the busy clack-clackering of typewriters and the shrill birdlike call of telephones Kristian often thought that if he wasn't going to be a sculptor he'd like to be a newspaperman.

Svante Jensen left the boys in the city room and knocked on the door of the managing editor's office.

"I've a list of people here who haven't phones or shouldn't be contacted by phone," Svante Jensen said. "And I have three boys who need bicycles."

"One of them of course is your young son." The editor smiled at his best crime reporter. "I've some bicycles ready below for as many boys as you can find to carry the message."

"I'll have to go to Helsingor tonight," Svante said. "Has the transportation to Sweden been arranged?"

"Yes. I've been in touch. Empty freight cars. But you'll have to do something about the children, the little ones. To keep them quiet."

"I've left my friend Dr. Holstein at a hospital where they'll give him the necessary drugs and help if he thinks he needs it."

"Holstein? Will he be safe?"

"He wants to help. He says we Danes are being very possessive about our Jews, thinking we can do it all by ourselves." They laughed together. "Anyhow, I've told him to call himself Jensen, my cousin, if he's picked up."

"God help us all," said the editor. "What times we live in!"

The three boys bicycled off together. Kristian knew central Copenhagen very well; he had lived there most of his life. Torsten knew that quite a few people they were to see either would know his father or about his father, because his grandfather had been the famous doctor. Thor felt for a time he was quite useless. Then he remembered that the other two were still young despite their confidence. Nothing horrible had ever happened to them, nor had they really known the facts of war. Should anything desperate happen, at least he had some experience. He would have to be the one to figure out how they could get away, even if he had to stay and fight.

The first place they stopped was a large popular men's tailor shop. There were over thirty people employed there, nearly everyone Jewish. The manager looked surprised to see the three boys. Then he recognized Torsten.

"How is your father, young man? Are you going to order your suits with us yourself now?"

Thor said, "Perhaps Torsten could discuss it in your office, sir."

Once in the paneled office Torsten said, "Please, Mr. Meyer, all I am supposed to say is would you please give all your people a holiday from noon onward. You should pick up your families and then all of you should go to the beaches near Helsingor for a picnic."

"What's all this, what's all this?" Mr. Meyer said impatiently.

"Tonight the Germans are raiding Jewish homes all over Denmark," Thor said. "You must get away. That is the message. Get to Helsingor by evening."

"My father is Svante Jensen, the newspaperman," Kristian said. "He sends this message. Please believe it."

"Hmm. Ahaa, *ja, ja,* indeed," said Mr. Meyer. "There is no reason why we should not have a picnic. Should anyone ask about it, I shall say we have been planning it for a long time."

"And everyone's family. Everyone's!" Torsten said.

"With as little luggage as possible, that's what Uncle Svante said," Thor added. "It must not look as though you were going away for a long time, just for a picnic."

Next they stopped at a small bank. The banker was an important man. He said he had no time for boys. They had no business coming into his office anyhow. He only saw people by appointment. He was a busy man.

"Will you please call this number," Thor said, sounding older than he was. It was a telephone number Uncle Svante had given him for just such an emergency as this.

The boys wouldn't leave. The banker had no alternative but to telephone to get rid of them. He listened. He hummed and hawed.

"This is ridiculous," he said finally, looking angry. "But under the circumstances I shall tell the people I employ they may leave, and if they are as gullible as some people seem to be, to meet at this hospital chapel. Ridiculous!"

"There will be transportation there to take them farther on," Thor explained.

"I myself, of course, will stay here. One doesn't just shut up a *bank*."

"But please send your family away," Kristian begged. He kept thinking of the people at Gormsgaard the night before.

"My family and I are going to the synagogue tonight as we always do for this holiday," the banker said firmly.

The next three visits were very difficult.

In the first house there was a nice woman preparing a festive dinner. The living room and dining room shone as though everything had been cleaned for Christmas, Kristian thought. In the kitchen there were preparations for all sorts of good things to eat.

"I've been saving for months, all the good things, for tonight," said the busy little woman happily. "On the eve of Rosh Hashanah we feast the New Year. Here, boys, have some of my cookies and tell me what I can do for you."

They let Torsten do the talking. He found it very

difficult. When he had explained, there were tears rolling down the round pink cheeks of the woman who had been so busy and happy when they came in.

"I believe you, children," she said. "Our friends would not send their children to warn us if the danger wasn't really there. But I'll have to wait here until my sons come back from school, and my daughter from work, and my husband from his office. Thank you, yes, I'll know where to go."

"Please telephone everyone you can think of, friends and acquaintances," Thor said. "But only say that tonight they must not be at home. If there is a buzzing noise on the telephone don't mention the train to Køge. Try to get that message to them some other way. And as soon as your family is at home go to the station and take the train."

"How long will we be gone?"

"We don't know," said the boys unhappily.

"What will we do when we get to Køge?"

"There'll be someone to meet you," Torsten said. "They'll tell you."

"My Aunt Minna, perhaps," said Kristian, swallowing tears. "She's a very nice aunt."

At the next address on their list there was a refugee Jewish family. They had escaped from Germany three years ago. When they heard that they would again have to move, leave the little home they had made for themselves on a small street in Copenhagen, they broke down. The grandmother, mother, the aunts, the children all cried. Their fear and sorrow mounted with their wailing and weeping.

This time Thor used the telephone number.

"All right, boys," an unknown voice at the other end said, "we'll take over from here. We'll send a car for them, and someone to help them pack a little. Poor people, you can't blame them. Now you three break up, try to speak to as many people as you can. Report back before five o'clock."

As Kristian bicycled on to the next address on his list he thought he had never been so unhappy before in his life. What if people, boys on bicycles, came to Gormsgaard and told him that the whole family had to pick up a toothbrush, perhaps a pair of shoes and pajamas, and go away. What would *he* feel like?

What would Grandfather Gorm say? He'd roar. He wouldn't go. He would shout he was a Dane of Danish blood.

Well. All these people were Danish as well. They might have come to Denmark later than the Gormsgaard family, but they were Danes. Father had said that while there was still slavery in the United States, the Danish parliament had passed a bill making *all* racial and religious discriminations punishable by law. He remembered those words. They had impressed him. They sounded noble. And long before that, his father had said Danes had accepted people just as they were. If anyone committed a crime they were punished. If they behaved so that they did not in any way hurt their fellow Danes, they could do what they wanted. It came to Kristian, as he bicycled, lonely, frightened and very sad, that at last he understood what his father had told him. It was a proud thing to be a Dane.

But the most reassuring thought was that he wasn't really alone.

He and Thor and Torsten weren't the only boys on bicycles going around Denmark telling people this unhappy news. All over Copenhagen and Zealand, Jutland, Funen and Falster and on the roads and streets and paths of the other well-loved islands of their homeland, there surely must be boys just like him, warning their neighbors of danger.

What a dreadful message to bring, Kristian thought, to say at a sort of a New Year's Eve, "Do not stay in your own home tonight."

On Christmas what would it feel like, he thought, if someone came to us and said, "Do not go to church." Synagogue was the name of the church Nina and Torsten went to.

When everyone came home to Denmark, he thought, he would make them presents, twice each

Christmas. And Karen could write stories for the little children.

He swallowed hard and bicycled on.

This must be the house.

It was a six-story apartment building. The people he wanted lived in the basement apartment. He went down the hall and knocked.

A girl smaller and younger than he opened the door. Behind her there were smaller children.

Kristian counted, "There are six of you? Or seven?"

The girl smiled back. "We sure never get to be lonely in this family. Did you knock on the right door, or did you want to know something? My father's in the hospital. He broke his leg. He's the superintendent for this building."

"Silverstein?" Kristian asked. "May I speak to your mother?"

"She isn't home from work," the girl said. She began to look worried.

"What does the boy want, Anneli?" A head peered over the first-floor landing.

Kristian ran up the steps, feeling relieved. Now he wouldn't have to tell the bad news to the little girl. He didn't think he could have, anyhow.

A pleasant plump woman in a big white apron took one look at Kristian and smiled. Most people smiled at him, particularly when he was looking woebegone.

Whispering, he explained his errand.

He said again, "You see, they must *not* stay in their own home. My father said that most firmly."

"I did hear a rumor of this in the shops this morning." The woman put her hands below her apron and kept nodding her head. "The children are alone? You stay here, boy, and I'll see what's what."

In the next ten minutes there was much coming and going. Everyone in the apartment house came down, chose a small Silverstein child, hugged him and took him home.

The woman at the top of the stairs kept saying to each small child, "Now remember! This is a game! We are going to play that each of you belongs to a different family. Do you see, do you see? It's a funny game. If anyone asks you, you must remember: You belong to the Eriksens, you are a Munk, you are a Kjeldsen . . ."

"Why?" asked one of the smallest boys.

"Because it's a new game. Just for now or perhaps longer."

Pretty soon the Silverstein flat was empty and Kristian was speaking to the little blonde girl.

"Don't cry, Anneli. Don't cry. You wait and see, my father will make everything come out well in the end. Perhaps all of you will come to Gormsgaard."

The woman in the apron said, "Thank you, boy. They are good neighbors. Tell your father we'll look after the children."

After that Kristian bicycled back to the newspaper office. He had had only one more address on his list, but he had not found anyone at home. He was glad.

Somehow his heart felt heavier than the huge baskets of rocks from the seashore that he sometimes carried on the handles of his bicycle.

When he had told his father what he'd done, he found himself in a car. He heard a voice saying, "I'll take Kristian with me. There is no one to see him to Gormsgaard tonight. He may be heart-sick now, but in the years to come he will remember."

15

Denmark
SEPTEMBER 30, 1943
(Always to be Remembered)

It was already dark when they arrived in Helsingor. Svante Jensen parked the car under the walls of Kronborg Castle.

"This will be your longest day yet, Kristian," he told his son, "but let us pray God it will be one we can remember with happiness."

A policeman came out of the shadows.

He shone his flashlight briefly on their faces.

"How goes it?" Svante Jensen asked.

The policeman wore a Danish uniform. His voice was anxious.

"There are too many people, we haven't got enough empty freight cars. There must be over six hundred at the station, in the houses, on the beaches."

"How many children?"

"A third at least are children or babies."

"We'll manage. We'll *have* to manage. We can't send them back now. I'll think of something. Nils," he said to the policeman, "Dr. Holstein will go with you. He knows what he has to do. Kristian, please go with them. Just try to look cheerful and confident. That'll help as much as anything else."

"Won't the Germans check the freight cars before they go on board the ferry to Sweden?" Dr. Holstein asked.

"They've checked them already. You see, most of them are empty and are sent to pick up whatever plunder is left in Norway, or whatever the Swedes will sell Germany. There isn't much time, doctor."

"The young people are here," Nils the policeman said, "the ones you sent from the university and high schools. Splendid kids. They've brought a camp kitchen and have been passing out hot drinks and food. They've told all outsiders they are celebrating the end of examinations."

Talking, they had reached the station. In the waiting rooms and on the platforms there were crowds of people. Dr. Holstein stopped short.

"Dear God," he said. "Surely the Germans will want to know what *this* is all about!"

"Not if we move fast," Svante Jensen said. "There are always people at railway stations. They are not imaginative, they'll just think it's normal to have people here. In any case, tonight most of them have been ordered to Copenhagen to help with the arrest of nearly eight thousand people."

"Explain to everyone," Svante Jensen said to the doctor, "that the trip will be short, if crowded. The girls and boys will move the families into the cars as soon as you have given shots to the children."

Dr. Holstein was already saying to a frightened young mother, "Believe me, Fru Kirshenbaum, it won't hurt him. It'll just make him sleep during the trip. We cannot have any noise for a few hours, you know."

Kristian looked across the narrows and said to a boy his own age, "Look, you can see across. Those are the lights in homes on the Swedish shore. It's not far."

"No, it's not far," said the boy. "I'll tell my mother."

More worried than he wanted others to know, Svante Jensen hurried to find a telephone. What if Aunt Minna couldn't help!

The harbor master of the fishing village of Gilleleje, fifteen miles northwest of Helsingor, had searched and finally found Aunt Minna. He had brought her to the telephone in his small office.

"You wanted to speak to me, Svante? Svante?" she was saying. "What? I can't hear at all. You have too many? Isn't that wonderful! Yes, yes I think we can manage." She began to talk in the childish make-believe language she had once taught her small nephews and nieces. No German could quickly understand that, should one be listening on the line.

"Try to see that the people you send us are agile. There are several Swedish boats meeting us halfway across. We could make several trips."

The wind blew cold from the north as she went out and looked across the dark waters.

From here you couldn't see the lights of Sweden. It was four times as far across as from Helsingor. But the fishing boats were sturdy. There would be friends meeting them halfway. That's what friends were for.

She turned up the collar of her old coat and said aloud to herself, "What do you expect? Of course the wind's cold. Tomorrow it will be October."

In every house in the village there were refugees tonight. Most of the Danish Jews lived in Copenhagen, but Aunt Minna and her friends had tried to alert the ones scattered along the eastern and northern islands of Denmark. They hadn't reached everyone, but those who had left their homes that afternoon and evening filled the village.

"There is Svante, sending us more passengers," Aunt Minna talked to herself. "I must go and speak to the captains of our little fleet."

Blinded by tears and her anger, she had walked directly into a patrol of three German soldiers. The sergeant held her by the shoulders for a moment. His flashlight glared into her face.

After a long silence he said, "Mein Fru, we are *soldiers*, not the Gestapo. We were advised there were no Jews in Gilleleje. We are now going to patrol the roads, not the sea front. But be quick."

As Aunt Minna turned to go and stumbled, she heard the voice behind her, "But take care. Do not trust anyone. You have not seen us."

In the nearest fisherman's cottage Aunt Minna wrapped her arms around an old lady. She needed comfort as much as the old lady who was crying for the cat she had had to leave behind.

"The neighbors will look after him." Aunt Minna wiped her rain- and tear-streaked face and spoke firmly. "You can be sure they'll look after him. He'll be fat and healthy when you come home."

Just about that time, at a small port on Køge Sound, near Gormsgaard, Thor was aboard a big fishing schooner. It hadn't been able to come into the small quay and half a dozen men from the Jensen Creamery and students from the lyceum had been ferrying passengers to it by rowboat.

Thor had climbed aboard to help up the elderly couple he had rowed over on his last trip. The skipper was hurrying everyone, his voice gruff.

"Into the hold, into the hold. Step smartly now."

Thor looked through the open hatch. In the dim light of a storm lantern, he could see a forest of eyes staring up at him from below. There wasn't a sound now, not the crying there had been on the windy shore, not the chanting of ancient prayers. Just the eyes looking up from the darkness and silence.

"You'll be coming back home soon," Thor said with difficulty. His voice seemed to stick in his throat. "There'll be a few more people to come. Then you'll sail to Sweden. But welcome back!"

He rowed back to the quay where Torsten was ready to take his place at the oars. He wasn't tired, but he would be glad of the break; the blisters in his palms were really sore.

He helped people into the rowboat as Torsten picked up the oars.

Aunt Ulrika was on the wharf. "Two more carloads, I think," she said. "Will there be enough room, dear God?"

"I think so," Thor said doubtfully, remembering the crowded hull. "But the captain says to hurry. He's going to put out soon, or not at all."

In the black sea, the big fishing schooner was a darker shadow against the already dark-blue sky.

A car drove down the lane to the wharf. A child cried and its mother's muffled words soothed it. Axel Jensen got out of the driver's seat. His voice was weary but firm. "We are almost finished. Ulrika, you and Thor and Torsten had better go home now. Follow the side roads, and if you are stopped say you have been visiting friends and had trouble with the car."

He was close enough now to see their faces. He put his arms briefly around their shoulders.

"Cheer up," he said. "Just keep thinking that in a couple of hours it will be certain over four hundred Danes will have gone to safety down this one little lane alone!"

Outside the station in Helsingor Kristian stood with his father in the darkness of the sheds. He had watched as the underground workers slid open the doors of the freight cars and quickly helped in passenger after passenger. The babies and little children were bundles of quiet, drugged sleep. When a car was full a Danish customs officer would appear.

"He's resealing the doors," his father whispered. "The Germans inspected and sealed them earlier. They like to get their work done in daylight. Darkness is not always safe for men with bad consciences."

Then the ferryboat was pulled up into a slip so that the railroad tracks from the shore ran onto the ship. There were loud German orders. Guards walked down the train, banging on the doors, making the customary last-minute check on the seals. Kristian clutched his father's hand.

If even one person coughed, one baby cried, someone groaned!

The train moved slowly down the pier into the cavernous hold.

"Don't cry, Kristian." His father's arm was about his shoulders, his voice was a whisper. "They'll be coming home to Denmark one day."

16

Copenhagen, Denmark
OCTOBER 1, 1943

The special troops and Gestapo force had arrived from Germany. In Copenhagen harbor the transport ships waited. In the night the men in black uniforms, a skull insignia on their caps, had moved swiftly and confidently. They had the name and address of every Danish Jew. This would be an easy *aktionen,* and in the morning the Führer would be pleased to hear there were no more Jews in Denmark.

Werner Best, the German plenipotentiary in Denmark, was so confident of the secrecy and military precision of this operation that he had already sent a telegram to Hitler: "IT WAS MY DUTY TO CLEAN DENMARK OF HER JEWS, AND THIS IS ACHIEVED. DENMARK IS 'JUDENREIN.' CLEAN OF JEWS AND COMPLETELY PURGED."

The Germans moved quietly. The Danes were supposed to be difficult, and the Germans had been given instructions to act swiftly but to avoid clashing with them. They were going to get a special medal for this simple operation. The Führer has said that the capture of eight thousand Jews in a night was as good as winning a battle.

Most of the men liked their job. They had been trained for it. They were the elite guard. They had chosen to serve this way.

This was a good game. Many of them had done it before in Germany, in Poland, Czechoslovakia, Norway, Belgium, Holland, France. They'd bash the door down, drag people out of their beds or from their prayers, from their meals, baths or study. If a mother cried for a blanket for her baby, they were taught to shout, "What does a Jewish baby need a blanket for; why get it a bottle of milk? Get going! Out, out!" It was a good Hunt-the-Jew game. They got medals for it.

This night in Copenhagen they had been told to use vans, trucks, bakers' wagons, ambulances and fishmongers' trucks to fool the Danes. For some reason the authorities didn't want to have too much trouble with the Danes. They were more useful producing food on their farms.

A few members of the Gestapo were successful.

They got the head of the Jewish community in his pajamas. They got a family out of bed. There was an elderly couple who nearly died in their hands.

But the curious business about this operation was that many of the Jews did not seem to be at home. *Das tut nichts,* never mind, they'd be back tomorrow, after all this was some sort of a festival of theirs.

All the same, the men in black uniforms with the death's head insignia, the men in the gray and the green uniforms, doing their duty, were puzzled. Then they got angry as they searched the streets and suburbs of Copenhagen. Where were the damned Jews?

They tried to break into Danish houses and apartments next door to the addresses they had been given. They had been forbidden to do that, but they *had* to find people to arrest.

The Danes would not let them in. They stood at their doorways, unarmed but confident. "We've called the police. You can't come in."

Sure enough, a Danish police car would be there immediately, check the names and addresses and say firmly to the Germans, "You have no right to enter a Danish home or touch Danish citizens unless you have the proper papers and orders from your superiors."

This was true. They had been ordered not to molest the Danes. This was supposed to be a friendly country. Blast them, they didn't act friendly.

As the night turned into dawn, the special troops, the strutting Gestapo forces, returned to their barracks. They counted their numbers and found that there were several of them missing. Later a few would be found in the canals, the sea. It had been a frustrating night, little to show for it, and where would their medals be now?

There was a meeting in the early morning at Dagmar House, the building the Germans had taken over as their headquarters in Copenhagen.

Dr. Werner Best, who had promised to deliver eight thousand Danish Jews to his Führer that night, was screaming in frustration. After all, he had already *told* the Führer the Danish Jews were on their way to captivity and death.

"Last night you imbeciles made a raid, a carefully organized secret operation!" he shouted. "How many Jews did you march up to the boats waiting to transport them to Germany! How many? I'll tell you! Two hundred and two! Out of over eight thousand Jews, you brought me two hundred and two! Most of them sick old people who will die on our hands."

A German general who preferred military tactics to chasing Jews said quietly, "I hear they were singing the Danish national anthem as they were herded on board our ship. It goes something like 'There is a lovely land that proudly spreads her beaches beside the Baltic strand . . .' "

Werner Best banged his fist on the table.

"We will get the rest of them. GET THE REST OF THEM! TODAY!"

17

Gormsgaard, Denmark
OCTOBER 1943

It seemed strange, the comparative quietness at Gormsgaard after the few days that had not seemed real at all.

Kristian had worried about the people he had seen loaded into the freight cars in Helsingor, until his father told him the comforting news that the harbormaster of Helsingborg in Sweden had sent a message. It had said, "A well-packed cargo. Everything in first-class condition. We can take more goods of the same class."

However, while the freight train and the ferryboat had been an ideal way to get a lot of people out at once, the Danes knew they could use this method only for a limited time. The first night of the raids the Germans, confident that they would catch everybody, had concentrated on Copenhagen where the majority of Denmark's eight thousand Jews lived. Now they were searching in other towns and villages as well. Svante Jensen had heard through the grapevine that the Germans did not yet suspect the Danes were so wholeheartedly helping their countrymen. The Jews still in Denmark would have to stay hidden with their Christian friends until they could be transported to Sweden.

The Germans had mounted tight day-and-night patrols along the Danish coast. All Danish boats had to have complicated permits to put out to sea, even fishing boats which, after all, did bring the fish the German troops needed. Some refugee boats had been caught farther up the coast. The SS patrols had also smashed a number of private yachts and motorboats.

Dr. Holstein, who had helped with the babies and the old people during that first hectic night, knew he could still be useful in the evacuation of the deeply troubled people. "We Jews must learn to help ourselves as well as to accept help," he said, and the Jensen brothers, while worried about the whole family, admitted that he and his wife with their many close contacts were irreplaceable. The children, of course, were as safe as they coud be anywhere in Denmark, camouflaged among their friends at Gormsgaard.

Everyone must try to act normal, Uncle Axel kept saying, but of course it wasn't the old life when one used to wake up happy each morning.

It was very difficult for Aunt Astrid, who was not sure whether her husband was dead or still alive. No news had come about him for months. She had returned to Gormsgaard, bringing with her refugees who had been smuggled out of Germany.

One of them, a violinist whose hands had been smashed by the Germans, did not leave his room in the stable loft. The painter with the broken leg tried to be helpful in the house, but he was still ill. The cellist was pretending to be farm help but he didn't know a turnip plant from a potato.

Svante and Mai Jensen had gone back to Copenhagen, leaving the children at Gormsgaard. Aunt Minna came and went. Thor said she was carrying on dangerous activities and ought to have him with her, there was surely something for him to do too. After all, while half the Jews had been gotten out to safety in the first few days there was still the other half to hide and to help smuggle out. Aunt Ulrika went about her household tasks with a gray face. Uncle Axel came home seldom, and only for a few hours. He was getting thinner every day.

Once Karen heard him say to Aunt Ulrika. "I just can't eat. I'm so frightened most of the time."

"I know you have been to Sweden again! You know it's too dangerous now."

"It's not *that*," Uncle Axel said. "I'm afraid that I'll fail by giving wrong advice, telling people to come to certain houses, certain ports, only to find them betrayed. I *cannot* be sure that all the people are honest, particularly now when so many of the fishermen are putting up their prices for taking our friends across. That's why I must take my chances with them."

To Karen and Kristian, Nina and Torsten, their grown-ups seemed splendid these days. And it was a good feeling to know that they had been trusted with dangerous secrets too.

Thor was full of admiration. "In Norway we have deep fjords and high mountains," he said. "We've got secret valleys and wilderness forests. I'll show you all, when the war is won. It's easy to hide there compared to Denmark. Believe me, it's a miracle the way you have hidden your Jews.

"And I think your father is the bravest of the brave. Each day he puts his head in the lion's mouth. So does Uncle Axel. They keep on trying to find out what the Germans are up to next, so they can stop them before they start!"

One afternoon in that week of relative quiet Aunt Ulrika went with Uncle Axel to the creamery.

She had wanted to do some shopping and there was gas available only for his car. Thor had gone off somewhere alone, as he often did. Grandfather Gorm had turned on the radio to search for British news, and Karen, Nina and Torsten had come to listen. Only the BBC gave reports of Allied advances and German defeats.

The Danish radio gave daily reports of domestic events. Today they heard that there had been eleven Danish hostages shot, for a reason not given. There had been strikes in a factory in Copenhagen, people had been captured and charged with sabotage. A group of newspapermen had been captured in Tivoli Gardens.

"Not my father," Karen whispered.

"Be quiet," Grandfather Gorm said, "I can hear a car. Turn off the radio."

The children did not rush out happily at the sound of a car any longer. Karen, Nina and Torsten left quickly, and quietly.

Karen turned back. "Black uniforms! It's the Gestapo, Grandfather." She clasped his big hand. "I think one of them is Rudi Dietl. What shall we do?"

"The hidden room under the stairs," Grandfather Gorm said calmly. "Nina and Torsten must go into it immediately. Have we any guests?"

"Aunt Astrid's three friends, the violinist, the painter and the cellist. They are in their rooms in the stable loft."

"Kristian is in his workshop, isn't he? Tell him to hide them. He knows the place behind the chimney in the old kitchen."

Karen ran.

She did not hear Grandfather Gorm shouting, "Where are the twins?"

But Nina did. She ran back from the safety of the secret room.

"They're in the garden. I'll get them," she called to Grandfather Gorm.

She saw the black car of the Gestapo in front of the house. The black-uniformed men were getting out of it with leisurely arrogance. Soon they would be pounding on the door. Where was Thor!

Even the cook would have been of heartening comfort, but she had gone to her nephew's wedding, taking all the rest of the staff with her. People had to get married whatever the state of the world, she had said that morning. They had laughed—then.

Nina was halfway up the hill when the twins came tumbling down. They had heard the car and were full of themselves with the crisp air and happy play. To try to get hold of them was like trying to catch quicksilver. They had of course been spoiled because they were pretty and funny, and good most of the time. When they wanted to be bad they were unmanageable.

They tumbled through the willows. Nina called softly but they paid no attention. She hurled herself like a football player and caught Lotte.

Pelle went hurtling down the hill.

Lotte began to howl. Nina clamped her hand on the small mouth. Below, on the drive, Pelle was bouncing around a Gestapo officer who now took his hand. Another car had pulled up behind the first one. Half a dozen black-clad men slid out of it and marched to the front of the house, guns in their hands.

Kristian had rushed back from his workshop. Looking very small and blond, he opened the front door.

What am I going to do? Nina thought. *What am I going to do!*

Lotte bit her hand. Nina rolled them both over the hump of the hill, out of sight.

"If you aren't good," she whispered fiercely, "I'll clout you one. You just shut up and be good."

She couldn't get into the secret room now, not in the house nor in the stables. What to do!

Then she remembered the cave they had made under the leaning rock, near the birches. They would be found immediately if someone really searched for them and soon it would be terribly cold.

But she couldn't think of anything else.

"Come on, Lotte," Nina said, "we'll pretend we are homeless gnomes living in a forest cave . . ."

In the living room the tall blond Gestapo captain, holding Pelle by the hand, was saying, "Now if it isn't Grandfather Gorm himself, after all these years!"

Grandfather Gorm stared at Pelle.

"Kristian," he said, "take that stupid child out of the drawing room. I have told you not to bring the village children into the house. They tire me. Then bring schnapps for our visitors."

"I'm not *stupid*!" Pelle's voice rose indignantly.

"The game," Kristian whispered and pulled him out through the door. "Remember the game!"

"Whose child was that?" Rudi Dietl said suspiciously.

Grandfather Gorm ignored the question. His voice was cold. "So you have finally returned, young Rudi Dietl. Perhaps you have come to thank me for the years you spent at Gormsgaard? I am sure you did not come to talk to me about children."

"About children!" Rudi Dietl shouted. "And about Axel, Ulrika, Svante, Mai, Ingeborg and her Norwegian swinish family, about Astrid and her half-caste children by her misalliance to the Jew Jacobsen. I want to know about all of them. And about the many friends I hear you have been entertaining!"

Grandfather Gorm's bony old hands, white at the knuckles, clasped the carved chair. He did not reach for his stick. He did not roar.

He realized at this moment that he was the only defense against this leering, prancing, dangerous man and the twins, the Holstein children, the three broken and defenseless Jewish artists hidden in the old kitchen, Karen and Kristian. If his own youngest child, Astrid, escaped from her room in a hysterical rage she would bring disaster on all of them.

For the first time the old man realized why his sons had been afraid of his temper against an enemy like this. He took several long breaths. He made himself relax. He stared as fiercely as was his wont.

"Well, well, Rudi Dietl," he said, spacing his words. "You've come a long way since you came to us a small boy."

"You made me feel like a beggar! All of you!"

"I don't believe that, Rudi Dietl. You were cared for and loved here. We were sad to see you leave us. You remembered us too until you became a Hitler

Youth and then later took on the black uniform. Isn't that so? Did you not miss us, as we missed you, a small boy we cared for, for six, seven years? You ask me now about your Danish friends. My son Axel is at the creamery, as usual. His wife is with him, I believe. I heard her say at breakfast she would have to go shopping with him since the Germans do not allow us enough gas for our cars." The longer I keep talking, Grandfather Gorm was thinking, the more time there is for the children to hide anything that has to be hidden. God give me patience, please, and help me to control my temper, he thought.

He looked at the tall old clock in the corner of the room.

"At this time my son Svante will be just about leaving his office. He is your age, is he not, Rudi Dietl? Why don't you call his office? The telephone is there in the corner, the number is marked in the leather book because I do not remember numbers so well any longer. His wife . . ."

"Yes? His wife?" Rudi Dietl's bark wasn't so loud now. He felt uneasy. He had been awed by this old man even when he had been a happy small boy in this house, after that other war.

"And my sister Minna must be at the flat in Copenhagen. Surely you will have found out the number by now."

"What about Ingeborg! What about that daughter of yours who married a man who is on our list for instant death! We have been unable to find them in Norway! Perhaps you have their telephone number as well."

At that moment Thor stalked into the room. His lips were drawn back from his teeth, his dark hair fell over his forehead. His eyes looked glazed.

He stood behind Grandfather Gorm's chair, one hand on his shoulder.

Why did Thor have to turn up now! The old man remembered hearing about his troubles in Norway. Could he stop the headstrong boy from acting rashly?

Rudi Dietl jumped up.

"Who are you?"

"Torsti Jalander," said Thor. "I'm only related a long way off. I'm a Swedish-Finn."

"How long have you been here?"

"I've not *wanted* to be here," Thor said, letting his mouth drop open. "I was going to Germany to fight with the Hitler Youth, but they stopped me here. These Danes are no good as soldiers!"

"Why was he stopped? The Führer accepts every recruit of pure blood."

Before Grandfather Gorm could speak Thor said quickly, "They said I was ill. Can I go with you now?"

Rudi Dietl stared at them. Obviously there was anger between the old man and the boy. The boy could be useful. "You will start to serve Germany now," he barked. "If you do well, I promise you can get into our army. First of all, answer me: how many people are in this house right now?"

"Children." Thor's mouth fell open in a stupid way. He nodded his head so his long hair fell over his forehead. "The old man here. The others have gone away because of the sick mad one upstairs."

"What sick mad person is this?"

One of the many things that frightened Rudi Dietl was illness. Every cold he had he thought would turn into tuberculosis; he was a hypochondriac.

"One of the maids," Thor said. "She'll start screaming any minute again. She's been ever so friendly with the Germans in the village, the ones who came back from Russia with the illness. You know. She's all covered with sores, and she smells."

Was he putting it on too much? What would happen if this horrible man went upstairs and saw Aunt Astrid?

Rudi Dietl was on his feet. He could check about Director Jensen at the creamery, and he could find out about the newspaperman by a telephone call from the village. All he wanted now was to get away from here. But could he salvage something from this disastrous visit? His superiors had his report on the treacherous Jensens.

"What about that Jewish doctor and his family, Jalander?" He glared at Thor. "I know they used the Jew Holstein here as their doctor. Has he been to see the sick woman?"

"He's gone away." Thor stared vacantly. "Away, away, with all his family. I saw them go."

"How? When?"

"They took a train to Copenhagen, I guess. Or maybe a boat. I wanted to drive them to the German police headquarters but Herr Director Jensen won't let me drive because he says I'm sick."

"The Jacobsen twins, were they here?" Rudi Dietl was drawing on his gloves, trying to hold his handkerchief to his mouth. They must all be contaminated. Where was his bottle of eau de cologne?

"Not while I've been here. Can I go with you now?" Thor moved close, trying to make himself drool. "Can I go to join the Hitler Youth now? And sing the Horst-Wessel song? I'm coming with you, aren't I?"

"Keep away from me," said Rudi Dietl.

They watched the two black cars roar down the driveway.

Nina and Lotte, their teeth chattering with cold, ran down from the woods on the small hill. Torsten and Pelle came from the hidden room under the stairs. Kristian brought the painter, the violinist and the cellist into the house, once more, for the time being, a safe haven.

Grandfather Gorm rested his arm over Thor's shoulder.

"I have such good children," he said. "I am so proud. I have such very good grandchildren."

Thor watched the evening sky and realized he would have to make a very hard decision. Soon.

18

Gormsgaard, Denmark
OCTOBER 1943

The visit from Rudi Dietl was enough. Obviously someone had denounced them. The treacherous behavior of Rudi, the boy they had cared for when he was starving and ill and who had returned to try to ruin them, had served a good purpose. While he hadn't earned himself the kudos of capturing a nest of Danish patriots, he had underlined the warnings the Jensen brothers had ignored before.

It was just lucky he was a hypochondriac. But that wouldn't stop a thorough search the next time the Germans paid them a visit. And everyone realized there would be a next time.

It was a pity. Gormsgaard had the space to hide a number of people, the ability to feed them from its own farm produce, and it was close to the coast.

There had been other disasters these past few days.

A fisherman had turned traitor and taken his boat-load of refugees to the Germans. Several other groups of people had been captured, one of them hiding in a church.

The luck of the first days had been due to their awareness of the danger. People had been hidden in hospitals, Lutheran parsonages, wine cellars of big hotels, in shops, libraries and factories and in many many homes. People who had given no active resistance to the Germans up to this time all helped their Jewish compatriots now. Despite the strict coastal guard, ships and boats of all sizes slipped through the patrols, at night, in fog, in storm. To take a risk became a normal way of life.

The Danes at last looked upon one another with pride. They hadn't been able to fight the overwhelming German army, but when the need arose, they fought in their own way for the lives of their neighbors.

The night after Rudi Dietl's visit, Aunt Minna came to Gormsgaard with two men from the Resistance. There had been a message from London. The Danish council, composed of high Danish officials who had escaped during the past three years, had had a warning that several people were in danger of immediate imprisonment by the Germans. Two of these were Axel and Svante Jensen.

There was a meeting in the old kitchen in the stables, which was considered safer than the manor house itself. If the Germans came unexpectedly they would start at the main house.

A man called Lillelund said, "So there it is. You'll have to go, Svante and Axel."

"And my best friends have almost spit at me because they thought I was collaborating with the Germans," Uncle Axel said ruefully.

"You are needed in London. We must organize for Denmark's future and the Danish council needs businessmen as well as diplomats. As for you, Svante, there is the beginning of an excellent Danish news service in Sweden. They can use you there. You will know how to evaluate the news coming from home even if sometimes it must be in code."

"We cannot just leave. There's our father, our wives, the children."

"You have to. At last we are fully in the war, though our armies aren't marching. You are needed. Gormsgaard is known. The twins will have to go with you because they are known to be half-Jewish. Rudi Dietl is a member of the lunatic fringe. If he doesn't come back himself, he will send others. Your sister Astrid can be hidden in a hospital in Copenhagen under another name until she is well again. And of course the Holstein family will go too."

"I'm staying at Gormsgaard then," said Aunt Minna.

"Minna, I can do without your help." Grandfather Gorm stood up to his great height. "I will look after my own household. Particularly now when I am full of pride in my family."

Thor stood up too, nearly as tall as the huge old man, and said quietly, "I am staying too, Grandfather Gorm. I've got all the papers to prove that I am a little off my head and come from Finland. Together we can surely look after the children, the farm, Gormsgaard, and still have an opportunity to work for freedom."

"We have you on our list, Thor Eriksen," said the man called Lillelund. "We have a record of both what you have done and what you wish to do. It has been decided that you deserve the opportunity to join the Royal Norwegian Air Force. A passage will be arranged for you from Sweden to Canada where you will go into training."

"Canada is in no danger," Thor said slowly, swallowing. He thought of the clouds and the free sky and flying, flying. "Norway already has many boys to carry her name proudly in the skies. I think I am needed here now. At Gormsgaard we still fight on. Do you need me, Grandfather?"

"Denmark can always use the brave," said Grandfather Gorm. "Here at Gormsgaard you will be a great comfort to all of us."

They stood staring at him, all of them. He was tall and thin and dark and utterly miserable. Everyone knew how very much he wanted to go.

Nothing had been heard about his mother and father for months. The German regime in Norway was brutal; his parents could still be safe in hiding, or in a Nazi prison, or secretly shot. The last news of his brother Leif was that after a tour of duty in Britain, flying bombing missions over Germany, he was back in Canada for further training. They knew Thor's longing to join the air force too.

"I am staying here," Thor said firmly, answering the question in the eyes of his Danish relatives. With Uncle Svante and Uncle Axel gone, he knew he would be needed at Gormsgaard.

"There is a lot to be done in Denmark before the war is won," said the man called Lillelund. "Each day the Resistance is growing stronger. We won't forget you, Thor Eriksen."

The fishing schooner vanished like a ship in one of the misty paintings by the Englishman Turner. One moment it was there, then there was nothing at all except the ebbing tide and the flowing mist.

Farewell, Father, Uncle Axel, dear twins, dear Holsteins, Karen said silently. Please God, let them all arrive safely, first in Sweden and then in their separate destinations. And return home soon, and safely.

"Come Karen, we must go quickly," Thor said. "We must not be found here at the harbor."

"I'm coming. I do hope . . ."

"Don't worry. Look, look what I've got."

He felt the waste of time was worth it to make Karen smile. He unwrapped something out of a silk handkerchief.

"Do you see, can you see? Feel it. They are dried now, but it's the bouquet of lucky Midsummer flowers you gave me before the war. Everyone will come through all right this time."

Kristian was calling softly from the dunes, "Come quickly or Grandfather Gorm will be out looking for us! I do miss Torsten and Nina and the twins already. And everybody."

"They'll be back."

"Welcome home," Karen called softly into the mists across the narrow sea.

Thor reached for her hand and they climbed up the dunes.

Epilogue

Records show that by the end of October 1943, 472 Danish Jews had been captured and shipped to the concentration camp at Theresiendstadt in Germany. This included the 202 people who had not believed their neighbors who asked them to leave their homes the first night, or who had not received a warning at all.

The rest, nearly eight thousand, helped by their friends, neighbors and people they did not know, reached safety and survived.

The majority of the Danes sent to the concentration camps survived too. The Danes and Swedes kept up a constant clamor asking German officials where the Danish prisoners were and if they had enough food. It was not like the unforgivable horror that happened to millions of other Jewish people in

Europe. The Danish prisoners were released sooner too, because Swedish Count Folke Bernadotte made an arrangement with German officials that they should be brought directly to Sweden. That was on Friday, April 13, 1945. None of those people ever again thought that was an unlucky date.

Of course the buses in which they traveled had to pass through Denmark. As soon as they crossed the Danish frontier, in every village and in every town and city, there were thousands of Danes lining the roads and streets, waving flags and shouting, *"Velkommen til Danmark!"* (Welcome to Denmark!).

When the Danish Jews finally returned they found their old homes just as they had left them.

Their neighbors had looked after them and everything was dusted and polished. There were flowers in the vases and their plants had been watered. Their birds were in their cages, their goldfish swam in their bowls or pools, and their cats and dogs, the ones who were destined to live that long, were there to welcome them.

This is a true story of one small country. I think it is a wonderful one. And also I think that when on the fourth of May, the Danish people put candles into their windows, it is not only to remind them that that was Liberation Day. It means that perhaps one day there will be light again.

All over the world.

Author's Note

During World War II, I worked as a reporter on the Toronto *Evening Telegram* and interviewed literally hundreds of Norwegians who had escaped from their occupied homeland and were training as soldiers, sailors and airmen in Canada. I also talked to dozens of Danish officials who had come to North America to explain their country's predicament to the outside world. My mother kept a scrapbook of everything I wrote and I have found these clippings extremely useful. While traveling in the Scandinavian countries after the war, I learned to know and love them, and heard many stories of the war years.

When I began to write this book, I asked for help from the Press and Information Section of the Danish Ministry of Foreign Affairs and from the War Museum in Copenhagen. I am grateful for their co-operation, particularly in supplying me with pamphlets such as "A Girdle of Truth," which is about the Danish underground news service. Then my librarian found a book for me, *Rescue in Denmark* by Harold Flender, published in 1963 by W. H. Allen & Co., London, and Simon and Schuster, New York. I was able to check my dates and information against this interesting, documented work about the escape of Denmark's Jews from Nazism.

The characters in my story are fictional, but many of the incidents are history. I only had to imagine how these people would behave under the conditions which existed in Denmark and Norway during World War II.

EVA-LIS WUORIO
SELKEE, FINLAND
AUGUST 1972

ABOUT THE AUTHOR

Eva-Lis Wuorio was born in Viipuri, Finland, a Hanseatic seaport. She grew up in Canada where she went to school, became a newspaper columnist and later a magazine editor. Miss Wuorio, whose books have been published in half a dozen languages, began her writing career as a journalist covering all sorts of news, from earthquakes and wars to royal weddings. She has worked as a free-lance correspondent in Europe and North Africa and has done a great deal of traveling. From her wide-ranging experiences have come the backgrounds for all her books. The time she spent in Poland just before and after World War II sets the mood and provides the facts for *Code: Polonaise,* a historical novel for young readers which tells the story of ten children who formed their own underground against the Nazis. Her travels in Norway and Denmark contributed the authentic background and understanding of Scandinavian people which are seen in *To Fight in Silence.*

Eva-Lis Wuorio is presently living in Finland in two old small houses in the middle of a forest at Selkee, which is in the province of Häme.